To/
Paula

Enjoy !

Best wishes

Lilian Brooks

Dormant Magick: The Whitby Witches Book One

Lilian Brooks

This edition first published by Salpe Publishing
2023

ISBN: 978-1-7393222-0-5

DEDICATION

For John. For everything.

CONTENTS

ACKNOWLEDGMENTS

This book would never have been possible without the support and enthusiasm of my family, friends, and readers. Thank you to everyone who has helped along the way.

Chapter One – New York

I must have had too much to drink, I decided, as I stood in front of the sink. From outside, I could hear the noises in the bar – the music on the jukebox competing with the sound of the American football game on the TV.

Football, I reminded myself. *Not 'American Football'.*

It didn't seem to matter how much time I spent in New York; I could never make myself remember that. Luckily Freddy, my fiancée, still thought it was 'adorable'. Just another feature of a Britishness that still seemed to him to be slightly exotic.

Freddy.

He was outside in the bar right now. No doubt he was still engrossed in the game and hadn't noticed that I was missing – yet. If I was much longer, he would be sure to notice though.

Okay, let's try this one more time.

I took a deep breath and turned on the tap. Instantly, the flow of water seemed to bend at an impossible angle, curving towards my hand. I drew back, but this time I left the tap running. The water sputtered once and then resumed its natural course, splashing back into the sink. Quickly, I turned the tap back off again.

It can't be. Not after all this time.

I pulled a hand sanitizer from my bag and used that, wiping the excess off on a paper towel. Telling myself that there was no way I could have seen what I thought I had just seen, I left the bathroom, pushing my way back into the bar.

It was crowded, and I had to weave around a group of people to get back to the small table that Freddy had managed to snag for us.

He looked up with a grin as I arrived. "We're winning." His smile faded. "What's wrong?"

"Actually, I'm not feeling too good. Would it be okay if we watched the rest of the game at home?"

He shot a glance towards the TV, not quite quickly enough for me to miss the disappointment on his face. "Sure," he said. He managed to inject a sigh into his voice as he spoke. "I'll get the tab."

"I'll wait for you outside." I had a sudden instinct to get away from the crowded bar. "I could use some air."

He handed me my jacket from the back of the chair and stood up from the table. The crowd parted around him as he made his way to the bar.

I pushed my way outside, shrugging my jacket on as I left. It was early March and New York was still cold. I leant against the wall and let out a deep breath. As much as I wanted to tell myself that what happened in the bathroom had all been in my mind, I could feel that there was something strange going on. I hadn't felt this way in … years. Not since my first few weeks here when I had been struggling to leave my powers back in the past. Where they belonged.

Even as the thought passed through my mind, I began to notice something else. It had rained earlier in the day, and the streets were covered in puddles. There was one right by my feet. As I watched, the water in it seemed to move, subtly at first, as though it had been disturbed by something heavy moving nearby, but then more quickly, with a greater sense of agitation. It almost looked as though there was some unseen force working on it, churning it up from within.

"Ready?"

Freddy's voice took me by surprise, and I let out a small yelp.

"What's wrong?" he asked.

I looked down and realised that I had stepped in the puddle, breaking the surface of it.

"Nothing." I indicated my soaked trainers. "I stepped in the puddle, that's all."

He gave me a strange look. "Come on," he said. "Let's go."

It was a short walk back to Freddy's – our – apartment,

only a few blocks. But all the way there I was offering up a silent prayer to whatever deities might be listening that it wouldn't start raining.

Chapter Two - Whitby

It was late when I pulled the car into the drive. I was glad to be done with the long journey from the airport – it had been a long time since I had driven, let alone driven on the left-hand side of the road. I let out a long breath as I pulled the handbrake into place, checked that the unfamiliar car was securely in the 'park' position, and turned off the engine.

Made it.

The house was dark, and I tried to remember whether I had ever seen it that way before. In my memories it was always brightly lit. There always seemed to be some occasion that meant we had lights all over the house – Samhain with its pumpkins and candles, Litha with its string of fairy lights that criss-crossed the entire garden. *It never looked like this. Granny Bright always kept the lights burning.*

I sighed and rubbed at my eyes with the back of my hand, trying to wipe away the gritty feeling that had settled into them somewhere around York. *There's no point worrying about all that now,* I told myself.

I took the keys from the ignition and slipped them into my pocket, opening the car door and climbing out into the breezy night air.

My back protested at the sudden change from sitting to

standing, and I rubbed at it absently as I looked around. There wasn't much to see in front of the house – but I could see the lights in the harbour below, the red and green signal lamps flashing on the sides of the lighthouse. The wind was blowing straight up from the sea, and I could smell the cold, briny scent of it as it lifted my hair from my shoulders and whipped it around my ears. It carried salt with it, and the salt stung my face as the breeze hit me. I wondered for a moment whether I had been away for too long to make this work; whether living so far from home had made me soft. Even my skin seemed to have lost the memory of how to live in this place.

Pulling my coat around me, I made my way up the driveway, the gravel crunching under my feet as I walked, hesitant in the darkness. Shadows drifted around me, and I half-fancied that the ghost of my younger self might be lurking out there. I could see it all in my mind's eye – me as a child running up the drive after school, with my pink backpack hanging from one shoulder, me on Samhain bobbing for apples with Izzy, both of us dressed as whichever horror movie character we had been obsessed with that year. Me, as a teenager, stealing a kiss with Oliver whenever we were sure that we were alone, and Granny Bright wouldn't be there to see us.

Oliver.

I shuddered. It wasn't the idea of ghosts that bothered me – I've never been afraid of them, and besides, there was nothing but happy memories in this house. It was the sudden realisation that I had been expecting something different. Something warmer. I hadn't thought about Oliver in years – I hadn't allowed myself to think about him – but now, so close to where we had fallen in love, I had to admit that a tiny part of me had been hoping that he might reach out. That he might even have been here. I sighed heavily. It was selfish of me, I told myself. It was too much to hope that he might have forgiven me. And besides, Oliver has his own stuff to deal with right now.

And then there was Izzy.

I pushed the thought of Izzy out of my mind. I knew exactly where I stood there – she had made sure of it. Eventually, I would have to deal with it – there was no chance of avoiding her in a town as small as this one. But I wasn't ready to think about that just yet.

So. No Oliver and no Izzy. It seemed wrong somehow, as if I was trespassing on my own home, with none of my friends there to greet me, and the last of my family passed beyond the veil into the Summerlands.

The wind picked up again and I shivered. *Wrong or not, I'm going to have to get inside before I freeze.* I reached into my pocket and drew out my keys – still on the old keychain with half a heart and a faded image of someone from an old boyband on it – and pushed it into the lock.

For an insane moment I thought the key might not work – that the house itself might reject me as a stranger – but then it turned with a soft 'click' and I pushed the door open.

The hallway was still and quiet, but it was warmer than I expected. I reached out a hand and touched the ancient radiator under the coat pegs, and I felt a little residual warmth. I had been paying the electricity bill on the place since Granny Bright died (over Freddy's objections, and without quite being able to explain why I felt like it was important) but someone must have come inside and turned the heating on for me. *Cameron,* I knew at once, and I felt a smile drag the corners of my mouth upwards as I thought about him.

I flicked on the lights and blinked in the sudden brightness. The hall was empty. There were no coats hanging on the pegs – not my grandmother's green wax jacket, or her best 'going out' coat. There were no muddied wellington boots sitting on the mat, waiting to be hosed off in the garden. There were no high heels sitting – lovely and out of place – on the shoe rack.

I pinched the bridge of my nose. I had known, of course, that this emptiness would be here waiting for me, but there was a difference between knowing something and seeing it for myself.

I took a step forward and a little bit of dust rose from the long rug.

"Sorry, Granny," I said, my voice barely above a whisper. "I'll clean that for you first thing tomorrow."

Somewhere, the house seemed to stir as if in answer – although whether that signalled gratitude or disapproval, or indeed whether it was just the wind again – I couldn't have said for sure.

Slipping out of my trainers without bothering to untie the laces, I padded down the hall and into the kitchen. I had half-feared that my grandmother's pride and joy would be buried under layers of dust, but the heavy counters and vast sink looked as though they had recently been cleaned. Sitting on one of the freshly scrubbed counters was a packet of tea bags, a note and something wrapped in wax paper. I unwrapped the little package first. Carrot cake! My favourite. Next, I unfolded the note. I recognised Cameron's spidery handwriting at once – it was familiar from the dozens of birthday cards he had sent me over the years.

Welcome home! It read. *Coffee tomorrow? I'll be at the bakery at 12. See you then.*

In spite of everything, I found myself smiling. It was just like Cameron to leave food and tea bags for me – and just like him to issue such a charming invitation without really giving me a choice about whether to accept.

I rifled through the tea bags and chose a vanilla and camomile concoction. *Just what I need after that journey,* I thought. I hesitated over the tap before I used it to fill the kettle. Nothing had happened in a few days, but whatever had been happening with my powers was unpredictable and I would hate to do any damage to Granny Bright's kitchen. I held my breath, but thankfully the water behaved normally and I half-filled the kettle before I lit the small stove. There was probably an electric kettle somewhere around, but Granny had always said that tea tasted better made in a 'proper' kettle and I was inclined to agree with her.

While I waited for the kettle to boil, I pulled out one of the chairs at the kitchen table and dropped into it. Without thinking, I had chosen my usual spot facing the window. It was too dark outside for me to be able to see anything in the garden, but my mind filled in the blanks: the small, sage-green bench, the tiny apple tree that we'd hoped one day might bear fruit, the rows of neatly arranged healing herbs that Oliver had helped me to plant. It was, for a moment, as though I had never been away.

The shrill whistle of the kettle broke into my thoughts,

and I busied myself heating the mug and mixing the hot water with the little packet of tea. I brought the tea along with the cake, still in its wax wrapper, over to the table and I drank it slowly, blowing on it to cool it down. I broke the cake into small pieces with my fingers – offering up a silent apology to Granny Bright as I spilled crumbs across the table.

Finally, when the rapidly cooling mug was empty, and there was nothing left of the cake, I left the kitchen and forced myself to venture upstairs.

Nothing had changed in my room. The same blue-grey curtains hung at the windows; the same green blanket covered the bed. I knew that if I looked in the desk drawer, I would find the same photographs I left behind – the ones of me at the beach with Oliver and Cameron, the ones of me dancing around the Beltane fires with Izzy, our faces bright in the orange glow, and our hair streaming out behind us.

One look at my old room was enough to convince me that I couldn't sleep in there. And my grandmother's room wouldn't be an option either – if my room had been left looking like a museum then I knew her room would be more like a shrine. The old woman had been revered in both the local magickal and non-magickal communities, and it would be a brave soul that would have been willing to even touch Iona Bright's possessions, much less pack them away.

No, I decided. *The door to my grandmother's room is just going to have to stay closed for now.* It was one more thing I just wasn't ready to face.

It was the last straw, and my temper, which had felt frayed ever since I set foot on the plane hours ago, finally snapped. I was abruptly angry with the house for its emptiness, for sitting here like some kind of twisted mausoleum when I wanted it to be full of life and laughter the way it always used to be. I yanked the blanket from the bed in one sharp movement and stalked back downstairs. I opened the door to the living room, threw the blanket down on the old, brown sofa and sank into it, wrapping it around me. I was tired – more tired than I could ever remember having been in my life.

I sat in the dark and felt the anger drain away. It was replaced with sadness – a sadness that I hadn't allowed myself to feel until now. There, in the dark, with no one to see, I felt a tear trickle down my face, and then another, until I was crying, hard. I cried for the empty house and the woman who should have been living in it. I cried for Freddy who I had loved and lost so recently, and for Oliver who I had loved and lost so many years ago. I cried for Cameron who had forgiven me, and for Izzy who never would. Most of all I cried for myself.

And it was only when I had cried myself out, that I finally drifted off to sleep.

Chapter Three

I was lying in Freddy's arms. He was smiling down at me as he stroked my hair, and I knew in that moment, that everything was right with the world.

That was, until he frowned.

"Alyssa?" he asked. "What's going on?"

"What do you mean?"

"The water," he said. "What have you done to the water?"

And then without warning, it was all around us – leaking from the taps in the kitchen and the bathroom, pouring out of the shower, and overflowing from the bathtub.

"It isn't me." I tried to deny it – just the way I had in real life. "I'm not doing this. We need to call a plumber."

The water rose around us in the apartment. The windows and doors were all sealed shut and there was nowhere for it to go, nothing to stop it from covering everything. With all the clarity of a dream, I knew that we would both drown, and I tried to grab for Freddy, tried to find some way to keep us together, to keep us afloat.

It was no good.

I watched as he vanished underneath the rising tide. The last thing I saw was the expression on his face – the silent accusation – as he slipped away from me and into the darkness.

I woke up gasping for air. My heart was pounding and the headache that descended on me was instant and painful. I could still hear the sound of the water, ready to creep up and engulf me, and it took several long moments of panic before I remembered where I was – not in the overpriced city apartment anymore, but back in the small Yorkshire coastal town where I'd grown up. The sound I could hear was the sea.

The room was bright, and I realised I must have forgotten to pull the curtains shut the previous night.

I untangled myself from the blanket and made my way to the large bay window, squinting against the sunlight as I stared down at the sea. The tide was in, and the waves were rolling lazily up onto the sand. In spite of everything, I found that I wanted very badly to be close to it.

"You'll always want that." I heard my grandmother's voice in my head, almost as clearly as if she had been standing next to me. *"You're a water witch after all, child. You will always be drawn to your own element."*

I straightened the blanket and the cushions on the sofa, leaving it looking like a makeshift bed – but at least a neat makeshift bed – and then I pulled a t-shirt and clean underwear from my bag, and headed back upstairs.

I deliberately ignored the closed bedroom doors and headed straight into the shower. It took a moment for me to force myself to turn it on – the vision of water pouring from the showerhead in Freddy's apartment was still strong in my mind – but I told myself I was being silly, turned it on, stripped and showered quickly, the almost scalding water making me yelp as it hit my salt-scorched skin. I dressed quickly, towel dried my hair, and left the house, heading for the beach.

On a summer morning, the beach would have been crowded with tourists and dog walkers by the time I reached it, but this early in the season it was deserted except for myself and the silhouette of some other hardy souls further along the sands. I half raised a hand in greeting, and I thought I saw one of them wave back in a kind of unspoken acknowledgment between anyone who was crazy enough to brave the early April weather.

I followed the path down to the tidelines. Already, the waves had started receding, vanishing back to join the sea with nothing left but some seaweed and some wet sand to show for their presence.

I pulled my hood up to cover my still-damp hair and stared out to sea, glad to be alone with my thoughts.

The sea at Whitby was a steel grey colour, rather than the bright blue that I might have seen in a travel magazine. It seemed to me as I watched it that it had always been that colour – in all of my memories of the place. I felt as though it was more honest somehow – I had always suspected that those azure oceans in travel magazines didn't really exist, that they had been doctored to lure in the tourists. That was, until I had seen them for myself.

I blinked, clearing the salt water from my eyes. That girl – the one who had visited those bright blue, tropical waters – felt like someone else. Another girl in another lifetime. I was home now, and gazing back at the familiar, white-tipped waves. Nothing had changed. And everything had changed. Much like the sea itself.

The vastness of it, which should have been frightening, felt somehow calming. There was nothing I could do to influence a body of water this big; it didn't matter how out of control my powers got. This was all mother nature's doing – none of it belonged to me, or to anybody else. And nobody could possibly have any influence over it. I stayed and looked at the sea for a long time, marvelling at the power the rhythmic swish of the waves seemed to have over me, marvelling at their power to calm me when nothing else had worked. It was almost hypnotic …

My watch beeped, and I swore quietly, the spell broken.

Cameron. The bakery was all the way across the bridge on the other side of the town. I knew if I didn't hurry, I was going to be late.

It felt oddly difficult to tear myself away from the softly rolling waves, but I managed it. I set off back up the beach at a slow jog, heading in the direction of the town.

I opened the door to the little bakery. It had been repainted in a beautiful sunshine yellow colour since I was last here, and the owners had added a small bell above the door. It tinkled as I stepped through, announcing my arrival.

Cameron was already inside and waiting for me. He stood up from his table in the corner of the room.

"Alyssa," he called. "Over here."

The place wasn't so big that he needed to draw attention to himself, and for a moment I stopped to wonder whether he was afraid that I wouldn't have recognised him, but then he stepped forward, wrapped his arms around me, and pulled me into a hug.

"It's so good to see you," he said, letting go of me with one final squeeze. "It's been forever."

I felt it then, the tiny piercing pain that his words stirred in me, but when I looked at him, I couldn't see any trace of reproach in his face, and I decided I was being too sensitive.

"It's good to see you too," I said, forcing myself to smile.

"I've missed you."

"We all missed you too," he said, and although he didn't put any emphasis on the word 'we', I heard it loud and clear. "Now then," he continued, and his tone was gleeful. "Now that you're here, you have to let me spoil you a bit. What are you having? Coffee? Chocolate cake?"

I smiled, a genuine one this time, and shook my head. "No cake for me thanks. That one you left for me last night was amazing, but it'll see me over for a couple of days."

His face lit up. "You liked it? I made it myself."

"No way! Since when do you cook?"

"I started baking a couple of years ago. I started with the old scone recipe your gran used to make, do you remember?" He paused. "What's wrong?"

The smile had slid from my face. I tried in vain to pull it back into place.

"It's nothing." I waved a hand in front of my face, as if I was trying to shoo away a fly. "It's just," I paused and let out a sigh. "I feel as if I've missed so much."

I never could lie to Cameron. As an air witch, his powers lay in communication, and he always seemed to have the effect of making the people around him speak more honestly.

He made eye contact with the girl behind the counter and ordered two cups of tea. She brought over two pots, and poured them into mugs, taking her time over it before she retreated back behind the till.

As soon as the girl had gone, Cameron reached a hand across the table and gripped mine. "You're back home now. That's what matters." His face broke out into a smile again. "And we'll make up for lost time, you'll see. For a start, I'm going to bring you more bread than you know what to do with. You know, since you're apparently rationing your cake intake."

His tone was teasing, and I was about to hurl a friendly insult at him, when the bell above the door rang again.

I looked up and froze.

The two people in the doorway could scarcely have been more different. The man was tall and broad-shouldered with well-defined muscles that were just visible beneath his olive green t-shirt. His hair was longish – longer than it had been last time I had seen it – settling just below his ears in a cut that looked less like a stylistic choice and more as if it had been a while since he had bothered to go to a barber. He had the beginnings of a beard just starting to show on his face, and an attractive pair of soft, brown eyes. Despite the chill in the air, he carried only a light jacket, slung over one arm. His lips were parted slightly, as if he had been mid-way through speaking when he caught sight of me.

The woman beside him was petite – barely five-foot

three — and she was wrapped in a long, purple coat that reached almost down to her ankles. She had short, dark hair cropped at her jawline and coloured with occasional streaks of pink. A row of silver studs shone in each of her ears. Her eyes narrowed as her gaze dropped onto me.

I felt it as an almost physical weight. She might have been small, but Isobel Jackson had a presence about her that was impossible to deny.

"Izzy," I began.

"Cameron," Izzy said, turning her gaze away and pointedly ignoring me. "What's going on?"

"I told you Alyssa was coming back," Cameron said. His voice was even. "I thought it might be nice for us all to get together."

"Did you." It wasn't a question. "And you didn't think that it would also be nice to give us a bit of a warning?"

"You wouldn't have come."

"You're right, I wouldn't. And I'm not going to stay either."

Before anyone had a chance to say another word, Izzy turned on her heel and left, the little bell sounding again behind her.

For a moment, nobody moved except for the girl behind the counter, who busied herself pretending to clean, her eyes almost popping out of her head as she watched the scene unfolding in front of her.

"What about it, Olly?" Cameron asked.

Oliver stood for a moment more in the doorway, and then he let out a heavy sigh.

"Black coffee please, Susie," he said, inclining his head in the direction of the girl as she scrubbed furiously at the same spot on the counter.

She nodded back, without taking her eyes off me.

I didn't care. I was too busy watching Oliver, watching the way he moved as he came towards us. He moved slowly, carefully, his large frame squeezing between the tables in a space that had not been designed to accommodate someone of his size.

He reached the table and looked down at Cameron.

"You should have told us," he said, a hint of reproach in his voice.

Cameron nodded once, acknowledging the comment, but not apologising.

I watched Oliver as he sat down next to Cam. I could already see all the things about him that had changed – and all of the things that hadn't. His face hadn't changed much, except that he had gained a few more lines around his eyes – but I had always liked laughter lines on him. Oliver Green had been a man that laughed often and easily, and I liked that it showed on his face. He moved more slowly than I remembered though, almost as if he was bowed by some kind of weight, and I wondered whether it was physical tiredness – an early start at the garden centre, or a bad night's sleep – or whether the sense of unrest that radiated from him had more to do with the band of pale skin on the fourth finger of his left hand.

Cameron gave me a look that told me that I had been quiet for a moment too long.

"Hi, Olly," I said.

"Hi," he replied.

He wasn't quite looking at me, but he wasn't quite avoiding looking at me either. Instead, his gaze was focused somewhere around the top of my head, and I wondered what he saw when he looked at me. Was I still the same person he remembered? Had I changed?

I raised my cup and found that my hands were shaking. Tea slopped over the side and spilled into a small puddle on the table. I replaced the cup in its saucer with much more force than I meant to use, and it clattered as porcelain met porcelain.

"I should go," I said, rising.

"Alyssa," Cameron began.

"No that's alright. I've got things to do anyway. Unpacking and stuff." I realised I was on the edge of babbling, and I waved a hand as if I was trying to dismiss my own words as I edged out from behind the table. "It was nice to see you again. All of you. Both of you."

I thought I heard Oliver start to say something behind me, but I didn't stop. Without even pausing to shrug back into my coat, I aimed a smile in the direction of the goggle-eyed waitress, and practically ran from the place, the little bell ringing behind me as I left.

Chapter Four

"Ow!" I crawled out from underneath the television stand – an ancient looking wooden thing that took up one full corner of the living room – and rubbed my head where I had bumped it. In my hand I held four wires of various colours which, I was sure, I had tried every combination of in the back of the TV set. I muttered curses to myself, half-tempted to give the thing a kick. One look at the solid wooden cabinet was enough to make me reconsider and I settled for another curse instead.

The contents of my suitcase were neatly arranged around the room. My clothes were folded and piled on top of the armchair, and my books and papers were sitting on a small shelf. There had been plants sitting on the shelf earlier, but they had looked particularly unhealthy, and I was fairly certain that whatever was wrong with them was beyond my ability to heal. I had cleared them from the shelf and put them on the window in the kitchen. It was the sunniest spot in the house, and I had some vague idea that the sunlight might work some kind of magick on them. My shoes were on the shoe rack in the hall – I wouldn't have dared to keep them anywhere else in Granny Bright's house. The sofa was still made up like a bed, and my pyjamas were neatly folded under the cushions. I thought that it was beginning to look quite inviting.

I checked my watch. Not even eight o'clock yet. It was far too early to go to bed – and I knew that I would never have been able to get to sleep anyway. Not with the scene from the bakery playing on repeat in my head.

Nice to see you. All of you. Both of you. Ugh.

I'd tried to read, but I'd found that I couldn't concentrate. I'd caught myself reading the same few lines over and over again. *No,* I decided, *television is definitely what I want – a bit of mindless distraction, someone else's voice to make me feel less alone.*

Less lonely.

The front door rattled.

I froze. Every instinct in my body started screaming at me to get down on the floor where no one would be able to see me, to hide.

The door rattled again, and then the doorbell chimed.

I let out a breath. *It's probably just Cameron coming to check on me,* I told myself. After all, there was no reason to think that I was in any kind of danger here. I shook my head. *The last couple of months have got you playing tricks on yourself, girl.*

I made my way into the hall, slid the chain free of the door and flung it open.

"Look," I began. "I'm sorry about …" I trailed off.

Oliver stood on the doorstep, shifting his weight slightly from one foot to the other. In one hand he held a massive pizza box, and in the other he carried a six pack of beer.

"Olly," I said stupidly.

"Hey." He indicated the pizza box, with a nod of his head. "I come bearing food. Can I come in?"

"Uh." I was lost for words. I stepped back, opening the door a little wider to give him room to pass. "Sure."

I led him straight past the living room. If he noticed that I had been sleeping in there, he didn't say anything about it, following me into the kitchen without comment.

"Just on the table please," I said pointing at it. I half cringed as soon as I'd finished speaking. Everything about this felt wrong. Why was I talking to Oliver as if he was a stranger, instead of someone who had eaten pizza with me in this kitchen hundreds of times? "Thanks," I added, making an effort to make my voice sound normal. *Better,* I decided. "Want a beer?"

"Sure." Oliver's voice sounded calm, easy even. It was unchanged from what I remembered.

He opened the pizza box, and the smell of hot bread, herbs and cheese flooded the room.

My mouth started to water. I couldn't remember the last time I'd had a meal – not counting Cameron's cake the night before.

I put the beer down in front of him and turned to get plates out of the cupboard. By the time I'd turned back, Oliver was already part way through a slice, one hand cupped underneath it to stop the toppings from sliding onto the table.

He swallowed and looked contrite. "Sorry."

I forced a smile and said, "It doesn't matter." But I slid the plate towards him anyway and he put the remains of the pizza slice down on it.

I sat opposite him, and we ate in silence for a few moments.

Oliver nodded at the plants on the window ledge. "Looking a bit poorly," he said.

I followed his gaze. "Yeah, they've been a bit neglected, poor things. I thought the light in here might help."

"I could take a look at them for you, if you want?"

"That would be nice, thank you." The strange, almost formal, tone was back in my voice, and I took a swig of beer, as if I could wash it away.

"How long do you have? Before I need to get them back to you?" His tone was almost too casual, and I stared at him. "How long are you staying?" he clarified.

"Oh. I don't know yet." I tried to take another swig of beer, but this time I couldn't force it down and I started to cough.

"You alright?" he asked.

I tried to answer but I started choking again and I decided I needed a glass of water. Nodding, to show him that there was nothing to worry about, I hurried to the sink and turned on the tap.

There was no warning. The water shot out of the tap and arched directly towards me. I let out a yelp and jumped back, my t-shirt already soaked. With a loud curse, I reached for the tap and turned.

Nothing happened. The water continued to pour from the tap.

I let out an inarticulate noise.

Oliver jumped up from the table and rushed to try to help me, soaking his own clothes in the process.

"It won't work," I wailed. "It's happening again!"

"Where's your valve?" he asked. "Under the sink?"

As I stared at him, he opened the cupboard under the sink, rummaged around for a moment and then said, "Ah!"

The water stopped. I was so relieved I could have cried.

"It's just a washer on the tap," he said. "I can come by and change it for you tomorrow."

"Oh." I buried my face in my hands.

"It's not that big a deal. It's an old house, there was bound to be a few things that needed some work."

I nodded without looking up. "Thank you," I said into my hands, my voice muffled.

He was silent for a moment, and then he asked, "What did you mean when you said it was happening 'again'? I get the feeling you're not talking about the plumbing."

"No," I said, uncovering my face, even though the last thing I wanted in that moment was to look at him. "I've been having problems with my … powers. There's something wrong with them."

He frowned. "I thought Cameron said you stopped using your magick."

"I did." *Was it my imagination, or did he flinch when I said that?* "Or at least, I tried to. But they just sort of started up again on their own."

"Like when we were kids?"

I almost smiled at the memory. It's common for teenagers to have problems controlling their powers; the sudden changes to their hormones can wreak havoc with them. It's one of the many reasons that witches tend to band together; it takes a village – or in our case, a coven – to raise a child. This wasn't anything like that though. At least then I had known what was going on.

I shook my head. "Much worse than that. This isn't like trying a spell and having it go a bit wrong. This is like my magick going haywire when I wasn't even trying to use it.

Sometimes when I wasn't even awake." I broke off, trying to banish the image of the overflowing water – and Freddy's face – from my mind.

"I've never heard of anything like that," Oliver said. "But I don't have any experience of witches who stop using their powers either."

He sounded calm, but I heard the unspoken rebuke in his voice.

I opened my mouth to snap at him, but then I stopped. I wasn't really angry with Oliver – he was right after all. I was just tired. And afraid.

"Of course you don't," I muttered. "Why would you?"

To my horror, I felt a tear spill over my lashes and splash down on my cheek.

Oliver looked stricken. "I'm sorry," he said. "I didn't mean to upset you." He stood and fumbled me into an awkward hug, wrapping his large frame around me.

I breathed in the scent of him. It was sweet and earthy, almost spicy. It was the same scent I remembered from so many years ago – the same scent I sometimes used to convince myself that I could still smell even when I moved away. It was the smell of an earth witch – but more than that – of Oliver.

"It'll be okay," he said. "The kitchen is fine. Nothing happened."

And I lost it.

"But it has," I wailed, like a hurt child. "I lost control of my powers, I flooded my apartment, I lost my whole life. I lost Freddy."

I could have bitten off my tongue the moment I said it. All the air seemed to go out of the room and Oliver froze, his arms no longer holding me, but instead going stiff at his sides.

"Freddy?"

"He was my … my …" I couldn't bring myself to say it.

"Your boyfriend?"

I sniffed back more tears. "Fiancée."

"I see." He let go of me and took another step back.

I wanted to protest that Oliver was the one who had gone and married someone else, but how could I? I knew full well that I was the one who had left him. Did I think he would wait for me forever?

"Oliver," I said instead. "I'm sorry. I didn't mean -"

He held up a hand to stop me.

"I'm sorry about your powers," he said, his face a mask of calm. "I can see how that must have been frightening for you, and why it would drive you back here. And I'll talk to the others about helping you out with that. But we —" the mask slipped and for a moment I saw some of the anger beneath it, some of the pain, "we cannot talk about your ex.

If you need to vent about him, or whatever then you'll have to talk to Cameron. Or to Izzy. Not to me."

I bit back my first reaction - which was to tell him that Izzy was even less likely to want to discuss Freddy than he was – and I nodded instead.

"I'm sorry," I said again. "I shouldn't have —"

"No," he said. "You shouldn't." He sighed, and some of the tension went out of his shoulders. Almost too softly for me to hear, he said, "I can't, Lyssa."

I wanted to reach for him, to wrap my arms around him this time, but I stopped myself. Instead, I nodded, once, and said, "Thank you for the food. And for helping me."

And despite the fact we both knew that there was more to say, he nodded back and said, "You're welcome."

I remained sitting at the kitchen table for a long time after he left, staring at the small flecks of soil that was all that was left of the plants he had taken with him. The smell of him – sweet and earthy – hung in the air, and I breathed it in for a long time before I went back into the living room, wrapped the blanket around myself and settled in for a long, wakeful – but thankfully dreamless – night.

Chapter Five

Cameron's shop was buzzing with a warm kind of energy when I opened the door. He had named it 'The Wayfarer' and the name suited the bohemian energy of the place perfectly.

It was so busy inside that I couldn't see him at first, but then I spotted him, hidden by a group of people standing in front of the counter.

"Great choice." He was talking to a woman dressed all in black and holding a slender silver chain with a pale blue orb dangling from one end. "It'll look amazing against that blue dress you have."

He looked up, caught sight of me and gave me a little wave, before he turned back to his customers.

I took the opportunity to have a look around the shop. It was the first time I had seen the place, and I was curious about it. Cameron had decorated it in pale teals and greys that perfectly picked out the colour of the sea, just visible through the large front window. The space was filled with examples of Cameron's work; silver necklaces hung from delicate hooks in the walls, rings set with smooth, shiny gems sat snugly in display cabinets, and earrings sparkled on top of soft, velvet cushions. The whole place was light and airy – and I loved it straight away.

The woman in the black dress finished paying for her necklace, flashed Cameron a smile, and eased her way out of the crowd, slipping the orb around her neck as she moved. She shot me a curious glance as she passed, and I felt the tell-tale prickle on the back of my neck – a sign that I was in the presence of magick.

I smiled at the woman, and she gave me a nod – more courteous than friendly – and then she slipped out of the shop.

When the place finally emptied, Cameron wiped one hand across his brow in an exaggerated gesture.

"Phew," he said. "That was intense. Let's get a brew and chat while it's quiet, shall we?"

He lifted a section of the counter-top, letting me through, and led me to a small room at the back of the shop.

"Have a seat," he said, gesturing to the only chair in the room – an ancient armchair that had seen better days. "Tea?" he asked, already pulling mugs from a cupboard.

"Yes please," I said, lowering myself cautiously into the chair. Luckily, it was more comfortable than it looked. "Who was the woman in the black dress who bought the necklace?"

"That's Heather. She's one of my regulars."

"She's a witch?"

He nodded, stirring sugar into his tea. "Yes, she's a solitary practitioner." He grinned at me. "Why? Did she give you 'the look'? Don't take it personally, she's a bit prickly with everyone until she gets to know them. She'll warm up to you."

I stirred my own tea. "Do you get many witches in here?"

"Depends on the time of year. In a couple of months, it'll be mostly tourists and the locals will stay away. Sometimes I do the odd piece of commission for someone in the magickal community though." He broke off and looked at me. "Why? Are you after a job?"

I laughed, but his face had turned serious.

"Actually, I have been thinking about getting someone in to help me with the shop. Not with the fun stuff, you understand, just with the boring bits – the admin and so on. You'd be perfect."

"Oh, thanks very much," I said, laughing again. "Nice to know you think I'm boring."

"You know what I mean. You're reliable, and you don't mind all that 'nine to five', routine stuff. Not like me, I get bored too easily."

"Typical air witch," I said.

He grinned at me and dipped into a half-bow. "Just as

you say," he agreed. "How about it though? You're between jobs at the moment, and I could use the help. Especially once the town gets busy again."

My smile faded. "I don't know how long I'm going to be here," I told him. "Izzy already hates me, and now I've managed to upset Olly again too." I sighed. "Maybe I was wrong to come back."

Cameron set the mug down on the sink. "Of course you weren't wrong to come back. This is your home; you would have been wrong to stay away if you were in trouble. And nobody hates you, they're just —"

He was interrupted by the sound of excited chatter coming from the shop. He rolled his eyes and groaned. "No rest for the wicked." Poking his head into the shop, he said, "Welcome! Feel free to have a look around, and I'll be with you in just a minute." He held out his hand to me, and said, "Well, what do you think? You can start right now if you like?"

I only hesitated for a moment before I took his hand and let him help me back to my feet.

"Is it always that busy?" I asked, as I turned the sign on the door to read, 'Closed'.

Cameron shrugged. "Some days are crazier than others." He frowned. "Speaking of, I understand from Olly that you've been experiencing a bit of craziness yourself?"

I felt my face flush, remembering Oliver's anger the night before. "He told you about that?"

He watched my face as he spoke. "Not much. He just said that your powers were on the blink, and you were worried about it." He pushed himself up onto the counter and perched there, his long legs dangling almost to the ground as he looked at me. "It was pretty obvious that he wasn't telling us everything though. So, go on. Spill. What's been happening?"

I sighed and gestured towards the back room. "I'm going to need more tea for this story," I said.

"And then he left you?" Cameron's tone was balanced somewhere between incredulous and outraged. "Your fiancée actually left you?" He put a hand over mine. "That complete and utter —"

"In his defence," I said, cutting him off. "I did flood his apartment. His very nice, very expensive, apartment."

"Good!" Cameron practically shouted. "It sounds like he deserved much worse than that." He broke off, muttering darkly under his breath.

"So, that's it," I said. "The whole, sad story." It wasn't quite true – I had left out the part where I had clumsily brought up my ex with Oliver – but Cameron didn't need to know about that.

"He doesn't know you're a witch though?" Cameron asked.

"Of course not. I mean, he knows that something's wrong with me but ... oh, Cam, no."

He moved his hand away, and I reached out and grabbed it.

"I'm so sorry," I said. "I didn't mean 'wrong' like that. I just meant, not like him. Like what he's used to. 'Wrong' from his perspective, not mine." I was babbling and I knew it. "I'm sorry," I said again, sounding lame even to myself.

A heavy moment passed before Cameron shrugged. "It's okay," he said. "The question now is, what are we going to do to get your errant powers back under control? Has anything happened since you've been here?"

I shook my head. "No. A couple of weird dreams, but nothing ..." I trailed off and waggled my fingers. "You know."

"Well, that seems like a good sign. Have you tried to do any magick?"

"No," I said, almost too quickly. "Nothing."

"Right then." He stood. "Come on."

"Now?" I squeaked.

"There's no time like the present."

"But," I looked around. "What if —"

He followed my gaze. "Oh, no. Don't worry, we won't be practicing anything in here. I've got a better idea. Grab your coat."

I shivered and dug my hands deeper into my pockets as I stared out over the expanse of inky, black water. Despite the darkness, and the accompanying cold, it wasn't late yet, and the tide was still out, leaving us plenty of space to roam across the sand.

Cameron stopped. "We should be okay here," he said. "Away from any prying eyes. Pull up a rock."

I smiled at him but remained standing.

"So, this is the perfect time to practice using your talents. You're right in your element here, which should hopefully make things a bit easier for you, and you don't have to worry about any, um, 'incidents' that might happen if we were indoors.

"Is that your way of saying that I can't break anything out here?"

"Basically, yes."

I gestured up at the overhanging rocks. "Have you considered the possibility that I might cause a landslide?" I was only half joking.

He followed my gaze and then looked back at me. "I think we should be safe. Unless you're going to tell me that you've morphed into an earth witch on top of everything else?"

"Not that I know of."

"Well, then. Perfectly safe."

I tried not to mind that he took a couple of steps away from the rocks as he spoke. Cameron knew as well as anyone that there was no such thing as 'perfectly safe' where magick was concerned.

"We'll start with something small," he said. "Close your eyes and focus on calling your power."

I frowned. "Cameron, I haven't done that in forever."

He shrugged. "Well, we have to start somewhere. And it's perfect for out here. If someone wandered up the beach and saw you, they wouldn't realise you were doing anything magickal."

I wanted to say, "No, they'd just think I was some kind of weirdo, standing on a beach with my eyes shut." Instead, I said, "Fine."

I closed my eyes. Instantly, I became aware of the cool wind blowing against my face, of the sound of the waves and of the last few seagulls returning to their nests for the night. I could hear music floating down from the town – something folksy with accompanying foot-stamping. Most of all there was the sea. I could hear the waves rolling out and back again in an ancient and familiar rhythm.

I sighed and opened my eyes. There was nothing supernatural about any of it. It was just the result of standing around with my eyes closed – the other senses always took over.

"Try again." Cameron's voice was gentle, but there was something steely behind it.

"I feel stupid. Nothing's happening."

He laughed, but not unkindly. "Did you expect it all to come back on your first try?"

I was glad it was dark so that he couldn't see how badly I was blushing. "Kind of," I mumbled. Without warning, a feeling of cold shot through me, settling in my stomach. "Cameron," I said, "what if I can't get it back."

I had never thought about it before, but standing on the beach in the dark, I realised that I had assumed that I would be able to call my power back to me if I changed my mind about wanting it. I had always assumed that it was an elemental part of me and that it would always be inside me, waiting.

Oliver didn't wait, some small part of me said. I tried to ignore it.

"Alyssa," Cameron said seriously, "of course you'll get it back. It's just going to take time. After all, you locked your magick away for years."

The words hit me like a physical blow. "That's it," I said,

slowly. "I locked my magick away."

He groaned. "Tell me you didn't."

"I didn't know what else to do," I said, trying not to sound defensive. "It's not as if I could have asked anyone to help me with it."

"But a lockbox spell? That's so … primitive."

"I was nineteen!" I protested. "Would you really have done any better back then?"

I could feel him staring at me, even in the dark.

"No," he said eventually. "Probably not. At any rate, we're going to have to undo it now."

"Can we? With just the two of us?"

"What, break a ten-year-old lockbox spell, cast by a nineteen-year-old witch, who only sort of knew what she was doing? Yeah, I think we'll manage. Was there a physical aspect to the spell? Any containers we might have to find?"

I shook my head, and then remembered he couldn't see me. "No. It was just a mental lock."

"That's one less thing to worry about anyway. A guided meditation should do the trick. Grab my hands and we'll get started."

I felt around for him and slipped my hands into his, grateful that he was warmer than me.

"Okay," he said. "Close your eyes and just follow the sound of my voice."

He started to speak, slowly and quietly, and I tried to focus on him, tried to focus on his words rather than everything that was going on around us. Once, I thought that I might have heard footsteps nearby, and it was almost enough to break my concentration, before I realised that in the soft sand, it would have been virtually impossible for me to hear anyone walking.

Just my imagination, I told myself.

I turned my attention back to Cameron, but something had changed. I couldn't make sense of his words anymore; it was as if he was speaking gibberish. At the same time as the realisation hit me, the sea seemed to get louder, increasing in volume until I wanted to cover my ears, to try to block out the sound. I tried to pull my hands away, but Cameron held onto them – without seeming to apply any extra pressure – and I found that I couldn't move

I felt something happen – as if some extra sense inside of me had started to come alive. It was an unsettling sensation, something I hadn't felt for years, but I didn't flinch from it. Reaching out with all my senses, I saw something seem to loom up in front of me, as if it was moving towards me from a long way away. As I watched, the shape resolved itself into that of an intricately decorated lockbox. I could see that it had something inside it, something that seemed to be pulsing with a pale blue light, that had started to leak out from under the closed lid of the box, colouring the air around it.

As I watched, the box rotated, until I could see that there was a slender, silver key in the lock. Without thinking, I reached out with my mind, and turned the key.

The box opened with an audible 'click', and silver-blue light spilled out, filling my vision.

I cried out and let go of Cameron's hands. This time, he let go too, and I pressed my fingers into my eyes in an effort to block out the light that was pouring into them.

"Alyssa," Cameron wasn't shouting, but there was undisguised concern in his voice. "Are you alright?"

"My ... eyes," I managed.

"Wait, I've got a torch on my phone. Let me see," Cameron ordered.

I turned towards him, and he gasped, pressing his fingers under my chin and tilting my face upwards.

"Your eyes are glowing," he said, and his voice held a kind of reverence. "Silvery-blue. The same colour as your magick. I guess that must mean that it worked." Even as he spoke, the light was starting to fade away.

I blinked, as the last of the brightness subsided. "And now?" I asked.

"It's gone; I can't see you anymore. They must be back to normal. Did it hurt?"

"Not exactly." As the light faded, my sense of panic faded along with it. "It felt strange though. A bit like having a torch shone into my face."

"And how do you feel?"

I considered the question. The roar of the sea seemed to have receded back to a normal volume, and the images that had swum in front of my eyes had vanished. Something inside me felt as though it had shifted.

"I don't know yet," I told Cameron. "Something feels different, but it's too soon to tell what it is." I stopped and pressed a hand against my temple. "I am starting to get a headache though."

"Come on." He took off his coat and wrapped it around me. "Let's get you home."

He led me, shaking, back up the beach and towards the lights of Whitby harbour, standing out against the blackness.

Chapter Six

By the time we arrived back home, the headache had turned into something more closely resembling a migraine, and I was shaking so badly that I couldn't get the key into the door.

Cameron took it from me, opening the door and ushering me inside.

"Right," he said briskly. "Up to bed, and I'll bring you some painkillers and a glass of water."

Without thinking, I headed for the living room.

"Where are you going?" Cameron demanded. "I said 'bed'." He stopped as he took in the sight of the old, brown sofa, made up to look like a bed. "Have you been sleeping in here?"

I nodded, and immediately wished I hadn't.

"Is there something wrong with your room?" Cameron asked gently.

"No," I said, with some effort. "It's just that it felt a bit … strange in there."

"Okay, well we can deal with 'strange' later. For now, you need to get some sleep and that lumpy old sofa isn't the place for it." He shot me a critical look. "No wonder you've been wandering around looking like death warmed up for the last couple of days." He indicated the stairs. "Go on."

Suitably chastised, I climbed the stairs and pushed open the door to my old room. I didn't turn on the light, but I didn't need it. My feet remembered the way. I flopped down on the bed, rearranged the pillow under my head, and was fast asleep before Cameron came up to check on me.

I woke in the cool, grey light of early morning. The pain in my head was gone, but a slight fuzziness remained – like a kind of after-image, as if I had spent too long staring at a bright light. Cautiously, I rolled over onto my side and squinted at the bedside table. A glass of water sat there, along with two pills, my house keys, and my phone. I picked up the water and drained the glass before I checked my phone for messages. There was one there from Cameron, as expected: "Feel better x" and then – my heart leaped in my chest – one from Oliver: "Meet me at the garden centre at 12?"

I sent him a quick text back to confirm I would be there, and then I sat up, confirmed that my head had definitely stopped swimming, and headed for the shower, feeling happier than I had in days.

I was a few minutes early pulling into the car park, so I took the opportunity to look around. The garden centre had been extended since the last time I was there, and there was a little café on site now. The place was a couple of miles outside of town, heading up towards the moors, and the day was clear, so I had a good view of the cliffs and all the way across to the Abbey. I breathed in the mixed scents of sea air and heather. It was just as beautiful as I'd remembered.

"Hey." Oliver brushed dirt from his hands as he walked towards me.

"Hey," I replied.

There was a moment when I wasn't sure whether I should hug him or not, so I settled for giving him an awkward little wave, despite the fact we were only a couple of feet apart. If he noticed how awkward I felt, he didn't give any sign of it.

"Ready to get started?" he asked.

"What are we doing?"

"I've got some spellwork set up in the nursery. It's nothing to worry about," he said, as I pulled a face. "It's only basic stuff. We thought it would be better to ease you back in slowly."

'We'. Cameron must have called the others last night.

I wanted to ask him what else Cameron had told them, but instead I forced myself to smile, and I said, "Lead the way."

Oliver led me past the café and through a side door marked 'Staff Only'. It was warmer in the nursery than it had been in the main part of the garden centre and there was a definite difference in the humidity levels too. I found myself wondering whether there were heaters and humidity regulators set up somewhere I couldn't see, or whether the change was a result of one of Oliver's spells. It bothered me that I couldn't tell – there had been a time when I could have sensed Olly's magick anywhere.

I didn't have long to dwell on it though, as he led me past rows of perfectly organised trees and shrubs and up to what looked like a large potting shed at the end of the nursery.

I smiled. There was a mild repelling spell on the door – not strong enough to make anyone feel actively afraid of what might be behind it, but enough to deter anyone from wandering inside. *Hidden in plain sight. That was definitely Oliver's doing,* I decided.

"Clever," I said out loud.

He smiled, pushing open the door.

Not even locked, I noted.

Inside, it was a little cooler than the rest of the nursery. Instead of potting mix and plants, the shelves held an assortment of innocent looking items such as chalk, twine, and paper. None of them were out of place in a garden centre, but all of them had magickal uses of some sort.

I was about to comment on the place, when I stopped, my attention caught by a hand-made book sitting on one of the shelves.

"Is that...?" I began, pointing at it.

I didn't need to ask really. I would have known that old book anywhere. My fingers remembered the feel of the paper, my nose remembered the smell of it. It was our book. Our spellbook – the one we had spent almost a whole year putting together.

"Oh," Oliver said. "Yes."

"I can't believe you kept it."

He gave me a strange look. "Why wouldn't I keep it? We worked hard on it."

"That's one way of putting it." I started to laugh. "Do you remember when we tried to make a vanishing spell?"

Oliver began to laugh too. "The night we turned your grandma's table bright green."

"And then we were trying to scrub it off when she came in." I was laughing so hard I could barely form the words. "I thought she was going to make *us* vanish!"

"It's come in useful, you know," Oliver said. "Not the vanishing spell, obviously, but some of our spells. Here, look." He took the book down from the shelf and flicked through it until he found the page that he was looking for. The book stayed open at the page when he placed it down and there were a few spots of dirt on the paper that told me he used it often.

I recognised my own, childish handwriting, and I started to read. "A spell to find lost things." I looked up. "Does this one really work?"

"Saved my ass a few times," he said.

I was suddenly glad that I had left behind something that was useful to him when I left. "Well, then you're welcome," I said.

He looked down at me, and I was abruptly conscious of just how close together we were standing. Oliver was close enough to me that I could feel the warmth of him, smell the earthy, spicy scent coming off his skin. I wanted very badly to reach out my hand and run it the length of his arm. I tried to take a step back instead, and found that there were more shelves behind me, barring my way.

Oliver cleared his throat. "We should get started," he said.

"Sure." I was relieved to have something else to focus on. "What are we doing?"

He reached down and took two plants from one of the lower shelves. One of them looked lush and healthy, its leaves a bright, verdant shade of green. The other one I recognised from my house. It looked weak and spindly, and what leaves it did still have were starting to turn brown.

"Energy transference spell," Oliver said. "We're going to see if we can use some of the energy from this healthy plant to heal the other one."

"Where are we doing it?"

"In here."

I frowned. "Didn't you hear? My powers are a little bit... wonky right now. This is a nice potting shed, Olly. I'd hate to break it."

"It's a simple spell. And we'll cast a circle to be on the safe side. You'll be fine."

I shrugged, trying to smile. "It's your potting shed."

He handed me a piece of chalk. "Do you want to do the honours?"

I drew the outline of a chalk circle onto the wooden floor, silently thanking the goddess that the steps had all come back to me. Without needing to be told, I automatically turned to the north and invoked the guardian power of earth, then east for air, south for fire, and finally west for my own element of water. I felt the circle close around me, encasing us in an invisible bubble.

"Nicely done," Oliver said.

In spite of the fact that this should have been witchcraft

101, I felt a moment of genuine pride as I smiled back at him.

He placed the plants next to one another inside the circle and handed me a piece of twine.

I wrapped the twine around them, being careful to add more layers to the healthy plant than to the unhealthy one, and again Oliver nodded approval.

"Good," he said. "Nearly there."

"And no explosions."

He smiled but stopped short of an 'I told you so'. He reached for the spellbook. "Together?" he asked, and I nodded.

With Oliver's finger tracing the lines of the spell, we both read it out loud and in unison:

"Spirits of earth,

Lend your strength to the weak,

Awaken the sleeping,

So mote it be."

"Is that it?" I asked. "Did it work?"

Oliver shrugged, bending to unwind the twine from around the plants. "We'll know in a day or two," he said.

I nodded, working to hide my frustration. *Not all magick is instant,* I reminded myself. *Sometimes you just have to be patient.*

"But hey," Oliver smiled at me. "No explosions. You want to open the circle?"

I re-traced my steps, thanking each of the guardian powers and letting them go, before I erased the chalk marks with a brush, and then I reached for the book, intending to put it away.

Oliver reached for it at the same moment. Our hands met over the cover, and we both stopped moving.

"I can't believe you kept it," I said again, desperate to break the silence. And then I said the stupidest thing I could possibly have said: "Didn't Gillian mind?"

Oliver went very still.

"I'm sorry," I said.

He was silent for a moment more, and then he said, "I told you, the book is a useful tool. Gillian is a very practical person."

That wasn't exactly a resounding, 'No, she didn't mind', I thought. Even I knew better than to push my luck though. Instead, I nodded and let go of the book.

After a beat, Oliver picked it up and tucked it away back on the shelf.

"Thank you for today," I said.

He nodded. "I hope it was useful." A strange kind of distance had crept into his voice. "You'll have to let me know if you want to do it again sometime." He turned to face the shelves and began to arrange the various items on them.

"I will," I said. "But your lunch break must be nearly up, so I should probably get going."

Oliver looked at his watch. "I'm a few minutes over actually."

"Oh," I said, "I'm sorry. I can show myself out."

"That would be good, if you wouldn't mind. I have a couple of things I need to get on with."

"Of course. I'll see you later."

He nodded without turning around, and I walked away, back through the nursery and the garden centre and back into the car park.

The headache had started up behind my eyes before I even turned the key in the ignition.

I pulled the car into the driveway and let out a sigh of relief. The headache was back in earnest and although it wasn't as bad as it had been the previous night, it was still enough to make me eager to get inside and lie down with a couple of painkillers before it got any worse.

I climbed out of the car and took two steps towards the house before I stopped moving. There was an unfamiliar energy – almost like electricity – crackling in the air. I gazed out over the sea, wondering if perhaps there was a storm on the way, but the skies were clear and blue. I frowned, rubbing at my eyes – and it was when I brought my hands down from my face again that I thought I saw something move – a kind of dark shadow that darted away before I could get a proper look at it.

I'm tired, I told myself. *I'm imagining things.*

Still, there was something in the air that felt oppressive, almost malevolent.

I drew my house keys from my pocket, and held them ready in my hand, forcing myself to walk at a normal pace towards the door. It seemed to me to be ridiculous to be afraid in broad daylight in my own front garden – but something felt out of place there, something felt like it was just plain wrong. I managed to get half-way up the drive before the oppressive force became too much for me. My nerve broke, and I ran the last few feet to the door.

The feeling followed me – almost as if something was giving chase – and I didn't dare turn around as I fumbled the key into the lock. It fit and turned on the first attempt, and I shoved the door much harder than I actually needed to, half falling into the house and slamming the door behind me.

I took a moment to offer up a silent prayer of thanks that the old key had worked first time, and then I leaned against the door and listened intently.

There was nothing. No movement. No one trying to

batter down the door or trying to pick the ancient lock.

I closed my eyes and listened again, this time trying to reach out with my magick. I heard the slight buzzing in my ears that always used to accompany my attempts to do magickal workings whenever I was particularly tired, or when I'd tried to stretch my senses further than they could reach. I stayed still and willed my magick to hold out just a little longer, ignoring the increasing buzzing in my ears and the sharp spike of pain that shot through my temples.

After a moment, I let out a breath and released the magick. The buzzing faded into silence.

Whatever had been outside, was gone.

Chapter Seven

I dug in the bottom of my handbag until I retrieved a packet of paracetamol. I popped two of the tablets out of their little foil wrappers and swallowed them with half a glass of water from the kitchen tap. I'd spilled the other half of the glass just trying to bring it over to the table, and my hands were shaking so badly that I dropped one of the little pills three times before I managed to land it in my mouth.

Cameron had left the blankets and cushions on the sofa. I didn't even glance at the stairs. Between the day I'd spent with Oliver, the unsettling presence outside my home, and the rapidly encroaching headache, I just wanted to lie down on something soft as quickly as possible. I closed the heavy curtains in the living room and lay down on the sofa with as many cushions under my head as I could find. I draped the blanket over my legs, closed my eyes, and waited for sleep to claim me.

When I did finally fall asleep, I slept only fitfully. A few times I felt as though I almost woke, but each time it was as if something soothed me back to sleep, and I could feel myself sinking back under.

And then, I began to dream.

The dream was the same as always – Freddy was holding me, and then the apartment started filling up with water. I couldn't stop it – I could only watch as my fiancée sank beneath the water, knowing that I would never be able to reach him in time to save him, knowing that he would drown.

Except that this time, something was different.

This time, I found myself in the kitchen, moving through the water, looking for Freddy. He wasn't there.

The water rose, and I sank beneath it, but unlike all my previous nightmares, I didn't wake up. Instead, I found myself in open water – a river, or maybe the sea. I couldn't see far in front of me – the water must have been very deep – but there was a pale, blue light coming from above me, as if the sun was shining down through the waves. I dived deeper, all the while searching for Freddy. Just as it was starting to get too dark for me to see, I caught sight of a figure in the water beneath me. I swam faster, pulling myself along in long strokes, already trying to work out whether I would have the energy to get both myself and Freddy back to the surface before it was too late.

The figure turned. It wasn't Freddy. It was a young woman, maybe a year or two younger than me. Her face was pale, and her long, dark hair streamed out around her. Her eyes met mine, and they were wide and pleading. Her mouth opened.

"Please," she said.

I didn't question how I could hear her voice under the water – I only knew that I could. I reached for her, but before I could do anything, I heard a loud beeping sound.

The dream shattered and I opened my eyes.

Daylight was streaming through a gap in the curtains, and the alarm on my phone was going off, the tinny speakers filling the room with noise.

I scrambled for the phone and shut off the alarm. And then I sat on the edge of the sofa for a long time, as I thought about the woman from my dream, and her bright, pleading eyes.

"What's with you today?" Cameron asked, in a tone that told me he was repeating himself.

"Huh?" I looked up from where I had been staring at the way a piece of sea-glass caught the light, turning it over and over in my hands. "What did you say?"

"I said, 'is anything wrong'," Cameron said. "What's going on? Are you getting another headache?"

I shook my head. "No, that only seems to happen when I do magick and I haven't done any today."

"Okay, we're filing that away for another conversation." Cameron mimed putting something in a drawer and closing it. "If it's not a headache, then what is it?"

"This is going to sound stupid."

"Worse than magick-induced migraines? Try me."

"I had a bad dream."

I half-expected him to laugh, but he looked serious.

"Tell me about it."

"Oh." I squirmed.

"Okay, so it's about your ex."

"It started out that way. I still dream about him sometimes." I flashed him a guilty look, but he just nodded, the same serious expression on his face. "This dream turned into something else."

Quickly, I told Cameron about the strange woman in my dream, the way she had asked me to help her, the way I had been able to hear what she was saying.

"And it could just be a dream," I finished. "Yesterday was kind of a strange day all round. But I can't shake the feeling that it means something."

"It might," Cameron said. "It comes with the territory for water witches." He frowned. "What was strange about yesterday? Did something happen?"

Before I could answer, the door opened, and we both turned to greet the customer.

"Come to the beach with me tonight," Cameron said,

when we had finished serving for the day.

"More magick?" I all but shuddered. "I really don't think I'm in the mood for that tonight, Cam. I need a night off."

He nodded enthusiastically. "Exactly. You need the night off. And that's what I'm suggesting."

"A party?" I lowered my voice, despite the fact we were the only people in the shop. "Is it a witches' party?"

Cameron shook his head. "No, just a local thing. A few of us have a tradition to get together this time of year, before all the tourists turn up and take over the place. Come on, it'll be fun."

"I'm pretty tired. I think I'll just go home and sleep."

"Alyssa, it's five o'clock in the afternoon. Come to the beach. Eat a burger, have a couple of beers, and if you still want to go home and sleep, you'll have plenty of time for it."

What else am I going to do, wait and see whether my 'dream girl' turns up again?

"One beer," I said, holding up one finger. I smiled. "Thanks, Cam."

I finished my third beer and pondered the wisdom of having a fourth. The veggie burger I'd eaten didn't seem to have done much to soak up the alcohol, and I didn't feel much like slowing down. From across the beach, I caught sight of Izzy eying me, and that was enough to make up my mind. I reached into the cooler, took out a cold bottle, and twisted off the top.

Izzy turned away, back to her conversation. She was talking to a girl with pink tipped hair, and a long tattoo snaking down from behind her left ear.

"Might want to go easy on that," Cameron said, indicating the beer in my hand.

I scowled at him. "This was your idea, remember?"

He just shrugged. "It's your hangover," he said mildly.

The beach was crowded and well-lit. There were at least two bonfires, plus a barbeque, and several tiki style torches set up around the place. Someone had hung pink and green fairy lights over some of the rocks, and they pulsed softly in the background. Further up the beach, someone was playing an acoustic guitar and several people were singing along and calling out song suggestions. Cameron was talking to Heather, the girl from the shop. Oliver was around somewhere – I had seen him when I was queuing for a burger. And less than ten feet away, Izzy was still standing on the tideline with her back pointedly turned towards me.

I suddenly felt the need to be elsewhere, to try to clear my head.

"I'm going for a walk," I muttered to no one in particular.

Cameron turned in my direction, but he didn't say anything as I walked away. I felt his eyes on me as I headed towards the little group of people surrounding the guitarist.

Up close, the music didn't hold the same appeal for me as it had from a distance, and I realised that it wasn't the music itself I had been drawn to, but rather my idea of what a beach party 'should' be. I only stayed for a few minutes, before I drifted away from the crowd again.

I walked further, until I found myself on a part of the beach that was largely untouched by the party atmosphere. There were no tiki torches and no fairy lights, no people crowding around and talking. A part of me breathed a sigh of relief and I wondered whether I would have been better off ignoring Cameron's advice and staying home. I couldn't shake the feeling that I should have been using the time to investigate my strange dream from the night before. Not to mention the feeling of being watched that had preceded it.

I should have told Cameron about that too, I realised.

I sat on a rock, finished off the last of the beer, and stared out down the beach, at the fires burning in the distance. It was peaceful there. Peaceful, and somehow familiar. It took me a moment to realise that this was the same place I used to come to with Oliver, Cameron, and Izzy years ago. We had chosen it because it was secluded, and we could practice our craft without risking upsetting the non-magickal locals. I didn't think I'd ever been here at night before, and I hadn't recognised it at first, but it was definitely the same place.

I thought about getting up and going back to the party, but I decided to spend a few more minutes where I was. There was something about this place in particular that I liked. It felt comforting somehow, as if it had retained the good energy that the four of us had poured into our workings together, all those years ago. If I closed my eyes, I could almost pretend that nothing had changed.

"There she is."

It was Izzy's voice. I snapped my eyes open.

Izzy stood a few feet away with Cameron and Oliver. She and Cameron both held phones, and Oliver held a torch. The expression on her face might have been one of concern, but as I watched, she smothered it with annoyance.

"I told you we'd find her," she said, turning to Cameron.

"Are you alright?" Oliver asked.

My head felt a little fuzzy, but I decided it was the good kind of fuzzy. "I'm fine," I said. "I was just sitting here."

"You've been gone a while," Oliver said.

It didn't feel like any time at all had passed. I looked around but there was nothing to tell me how long I had been gone, no stars visible in the darkness for me to track the passage of time.

"Sorry," I said. "I must have lost track."

Izzy let out a small snort. "See? She's fine. Now can we all get back to the party?"

She didn't put any particular emphasis on the word 'all', but I noticed it anyway.

"I might stay out here a little longer," I said. "It's nice here. I'd almost forgotten about it."

Izzy let out another snort, and it seemed that she was about to say something else, but before she could speak, a scream rang out in the dark.

"What was that?" I sprang to my feet.

"It came from over there." Cameron pointed.

Moving almost as one, we sprinted up the beach in the direction Cameron had indicated. Another scream pierced the air, and I ran faster, pumping my legs on the wet sand.

Izzy swore as we rounded an outcrop of rocks. "There's someone in the water."

"Can you see them?" I asked, gasping for breath.

"No. Just a figure. Over there." She pointed.

Oliver and Cameron were already removing their coats and shoes.

Oliver threw his trainers behind him as he ran towards the water. "Stay with her," he shouted, and Izzy nodded.

"Lifeboat," Cameron called, as he followed Oliver into the water.

Izzy was already raising her phone and unlocking it. Her face looked green in the sudden light from the small screen and her fingers moved quickly on the keypad as she dialled.

I barely heard anything she was saying as she spoke urgently into the phone. Instead, I found myself moving towards the water, as if drawn there by an invisible force. I could still hear the cries of the girl in the water, and I could just make out the two shapes of Oliver and Cameron moving towards her, but it was as if it wasn't really happening – as if I was watching it all unfold on a TV screen.

"Hey!" Izzy shouted, grabbing at my arm. "Stay here."

I barely felt it. Izzy, like everything else, seemed to have faded into the background. There was only one thing that felt real – and it was the most urgent, pressing sensation I had ever felt in my life.

That girl is going to die. And I can save her.

I wasn't sure whether I had spoken the words out loud as I shook Izzy's hand off my arm, or whether they were only in my head, but I knew that I had the power to bring the girl safely to the shore. I walked towards the sea, raised my arms above my head, and called my power.

There was no spell involved, no ritual. There was none

of Cameron's meditation. I simply spoke my power into the water, and – despite the size of it, the vastness – the water responded.

A wave rose up under the girl as she struggled in the water. She screamed again, but instead of crashing over her, the wave continued to roll underneath her, lifting her and propelling her back towards the shore. She washed up at my feet, coughing and spluttering as she spat water onto the sand.

Izzy's face was a mask of shock – her mouth hanging open, even as a series of sounds emanating from the phone suggested that someone on the other end of the line was trying to get her attention.

In the water, Oliver and Cameron had turned around and were swimming back towards the shore – Cameron calling out to Izzy as he swam.

I could hear voices on the beach, and I dimly registered that it must be some of the other partygoers, drawn here by the sounds of screaming.

It was the last thing I heard. With my gaze still fixed on Izzy's face, I pitched over into the wet sand, and fainted dead away.

Chapter Eight

I woke up slowly, swimming up from under layers of consciousness towards a bright light. When I opened my eyes, I didn't recognise the room, with its soft cream-coloured walls, or its grey blinds hanging at the window. I sat up slowly and pushed away a pink bedspread that someone had laid over me. My head felt sore, and I reached one hand up to touch my temple. My fingers came away sticky and for a moment I panicked, thinking it might be blood, but it turned out to be the remnants of some kind of balm that smelled faintly of mint and lavender.

As I looked around, I spotted a glass of water standing next to the bed. My lips were dry, and my throat felt as though I had been swallowing sand. I reached for the water and made myself sip it slowly so as not to be sick. I started to feel better almost immediately, and I swung my legs off the side of the bed, and stood, my hands braced out on either side in case I needed to sit down again quickly. My legs shook a little, but they held. I took one experimental step forward, and then another. Moving slowly, I made my way to the bedroom door and pushed it open. From downstairs I could hear familiar voices, speaking quietly.

"We have to tell her." That was Cameron, his tone firm.

"She needs to be able to protect herself."

"Can she protect herself though?" That was Oliver.

"After what happened at the party? Do you really need to ask?" Cameron again.

"But if something is happening with her magick, we have no way of knowing whether she could call on her powers again if she needed to."

"Shush." That last one was Izzy. "She's awake."

I swore inwardly, and then shrugged. If anyone would know about concealment, it would be a fire witch.

I descended the staircase, gripping the handrail tightly as I moved, and found myself in a small living room. In stark contrast to the muted colours of the bedroom, this room was decorated in bright shades of yellow, with orange and red cushions and throws covering every available surface. I knew this room – it was Izzy's living room. I was in Izzy's house!

The other three looked up as I entered.

"How are you feeling?" Oliver asked, at the exact same moment as Cameron said, "Are you okay?"

Izzy said nothing, but she continued to study my face.

"I'm okay," I said. "I think. What happened?"

"How much do you remember?" Cameron asked.

I frowned. "Not much. We were at the party, there was a girl in the water and I —" I broke off and looked around at them, taking in the expressions on their faces; half-curious, half-concerned. All serious. "Did I pull a girl out of the sea?" I asked.

"With your magick," Oliver said.

In a rush, the images came flooding back; the girl in the water, Oliver and Cameron swimming towards her, Izzy's face, pale in the light of her phone screen, as she talked to the emergency services. And that feeling. The feeling that I could reach out with my powers, the certainty that the water would respond to me if I did. That all I had to do was say the word.

"I saved her." I said it quietly.

"You used your powers in public." Izzy's voice was tight, as though she was trying not to shout. "You could have exposed yourself. You could have exposed all of us." She shot me a glare. "And you didn't even stop to consider it, did you?"

"I …" There was no way to tell her that I hadn't thought about it, that the whole situation seemed to have unfolded so quickly that there had been no time to think about it. "I didn't mean …"

"No." Izzy folded her arms across her chest. "I'm sure you didn't."

"She did save that girl, Iz," Oliver said quietly.

Izzy's face darkened and she opened her mouth, as if she

was going to say something else, but then she sighed, and her face softened. She suddenly looked much younger than her years, and very, very tired.

There was something else too. Something I had noticed on the beach, while the boys were in the water. Isobel Jackson looked afraid.

She turned back to me with an obvious effort. "You did save her," she said. "But now isn't the time for flashy displays of power."

"I couldn't just leave her to drown."

"Who said anything about leaving her to drown?" she shot back. "Olly and Cam were in the water, and I would have been with them if I hadn't had to babysit you! The lifeboat had already launched …" Izzy lowered her voice and shook her head. "No one was leaving her to drown."

I nodded. "You're right. I'm sorry. I didn't mean to suggest that you didn't care. It's just that I saw her there and I knew I could save her. I *knew* it, Izzy, and I can't explain how, but I had to act on it." I hesitated. "Besides, there was nobody else there. No one saw us."

"You can't know that for sure," Izzy said.

I wanted to reach out to her, to ask her what was wrong, but I had seen the way she flinched when I spoke her name. Despite the fact that she was within touching distance of me, I had never felt further away from her.

"We should tell her," Cameron said. He looked around at the others.

Oliver nodded. "It's time."

"Tell me what?" I asked.

Cameron dropped onto one of Izzy's plump sofas and patted the seat next to him. "I think you're probably going to want to sit down for this," he said.

"A witch hunter?" I repeated Cameron's words. "As in sixteenth century, tall hat and cloak?"

"Likes to murder witches," Cameron confirmed. "The 'Malleus Mallificarum', and all that stuff."

"But there are no witch hunters. Not anymore."

"Just like there are no real witches," Oliver said quietly.

I felt the blood drain from my face, and I was glad I had followed Cameron's advice to sit down. I risked a glance at Izzy, who was carefully focusing her gaze somewhere in the middle distance.

"We're not one hundred percent sure, of course," Cameron said. "But there have been some pretty disturbing rumours swirling around in the magickal community." He paused and looked at Oliver and Izzy.

"Tell her," Izzy said, without looking up. "She might as well know everything."

"People have been going missing."

"What?"

"Not many." He held up a hand, as though he could ward off my rising panic. "And not around here. But enough that the community has started to take notice."

"How many?" I asked. I felt numb.

Cameron ticked them off on his fingers. "Two in Liverpool last summer. One in York a few months ago. A few isolated cases in some of the smaller towns. People do go missing, especially in big cities – it's not that unusual. But when you throw in the fact that they were all witches…"

"You have a pattern," I said.

"Exactly."

"But what makes you think that it's a witch hunter, specifically?" I pressed.

Cameron's lips twisted, as if he had a bad taste in his mouth. "The guy who went missing from the York coven, Ian. His sister broke into his place when she couldn't find him, and she found something written above his alter."

"Oh, Cam." I knew what he was going to say before he spoke.

"Suffer not the witch to live."

"That's horrible," I said quietly.

"That's why we can't risk getting caught using magick," Izzy said.

I looked her full in the face. "You should have told me."

She stared back at me defiantly. "I didn't think you'd need to be told to avoid using your magick. You're the one who wanted to become a shade."

The whole room seemed to turn cold.

"Izzy," Cameron said, sounding shocked. "She isn't a shade."

"A witch who turns her back on her magick. What would you call it?"

"Not that." His voice was firm.

"It doesn't matter anyway," I said, and I hated the sudden thickness in my voice, as if I was trying to fight back tears. "I can't control it. It just sort of leaks out of me at odd times."

"That's why we're training you," Oliver said. "So that you can learn to control it. And to protect yourself if you need to."

His words were kind, but they felt like a knife to my heart.

That's why they're helping me. Not because they're my friends but because they don't want me to accidentally expose them.

And what's wrong with that? Another smaller part of me asked. Didn't you only come home because you needed help? Aren't you using them too?

Ignoring the competing voices, I forced a small smile.

"Anyway, it's just something to be aware of," Cameron

said, standing. "Nothing's happened around here. No missing people, no scary invisible presences following us around, no boogeymen down dark alleys." He wiggled his fingers in my face. "So, probably nothing to worry about. Why don't I sort you out with some tea and toast so we can start to build your strength back up and then we can … Alyssa?"

My face must have turned pale. Cameron's words echoed through my mind: *'no scary invisible presences following us around'*…

Oh, gods!

Oliver knelt down in front of me. "What's wrong?" he asked, his eyes gentle.

I swallowed hard, despite the dryness in my throat.

"I think you'd better sit back down," I said to Cameron. "There's something I need to tell you."

Chapter Nine

"You should have told us earlier." Izzy's arms were folded across her chest again, and she leaned on the doorframe as though she was too restless to sit down.

I rounded on her. "*I* should have told *you?* That's rich! I'm not the one that's been keeping secrets!"

Izzy's eyes bored into mine, and even after so much time apart, I found that I could still read the expression in them. *Haven't you?* she seemed to be saying.

"Maybe we should have told you," Oliver said. "But we didn't want to scare you off when your powers had just started to re-emerge. Besides, your home and Cam's shop are both warded. It was the most we could do without being intrusive."

I felt something soften inside me. "You warded my house?"

"I did," Izzy said, and I thought again that this made sense. Everybody knew that fire witches made the strongest wards. "I didn't want to leave you unprotected," she added.

I gave her a hard stare, wondering whether she was having yet another dig at me for leaving instead of joining with her and the others to form a coven all those years ago. Izzy more than anyone had wanted the protection that stronger powers would have brought.

Her face was blank and almost too innocent.

"Thank you," I said finally.

She shrugged and looked away.

Cameron raised his hands in a conciliatory gesture. "From now on, no more secrets," he said. "For any of us. It's too dangerous."

Izzy nodded.

After a moment, I nodded too.

"And I think," Cameron continued, "that we should stay together from now on. If Alyssa did feel something outside her home, then it could mean that there's something unfriendly in Whitby. Even if it isn't the witch hunter, I don't think anyone should go off on their own until we get to the bottom of it, okay?"

"It could be nothing," I started to say, at the same time as Izzy said, "The houses are all warded."

We both stopped and looked at one another.

Cameron smiled.

It was already dusk by the time Oliver drove me home.

"Anything?" he asked as he turned off the engine.

I closed my eyes and reached out with my senses. The buzzing returned – louder this time – but there was no sense of anything behind it, no sign of anything hiding in the shadows. "Nothing," I said. "You?"

He shook his head. "I don't feel anything. I'll check your wards out anyway though, just to be safe."

He rummaged in the glove compartment and pulled out a small, black torch, before he opened the door and marched up the garden path.

I followed, keeping alert for anything that might try to ambush us in the gathering dark.

By the time Oliver had finished checking the last of the wards, my heart was hammering uncomfortably in my chest. Izzy had done a thorough job – there were fifteen wards on the outside of the house, covering every possible entry point – and it had taken Oliver far longer than I realised it would to check them all. The effort of keeping my senses engaged for so long had left me feeling anxious and drained.

"All good here," Oliver said, and I let out a breath, expelling the air in a rush.

"Great, thank you."

"There's a couple inside too. Want me to check those for you?"

I frowned. "Izzy was inside the house?"

It shouldn't have bothered me. Cameron had been looking after the place for me while I had been away, so I knew that he had been inside pretty regularly. And Oliver had been inside since I'd been back. But Izzy. Izzy had practically grown up in that house – with me – and something about the idea of her being there alone made my stomach coil into a knot.

Oliver gave me a knowing look, and I was suddenly – ridiculously – grateful that he understood.

"She came in with Cameron, and she only put a couple of wards up in the entryway. We all agreed that you shouldn't need any in the main part of the house," he said.

I nodded and said, without thinking, "The house itself would take care of everything else anyway."

I stopped. It was the first time I had acknowledged – out loud or to myself – that there was something in the house, some kind of spirit or fae, protecting the place. *Was it always this way?* I wondered. I had always felt safe in the house – in my home – but I'd never really thought about it before. I had always assumed that it was Granny Bright's welcoming presence that had made me feel secure, but even with her gone, I still felt the same way.

Oliver gave me that look again, the one that said he understood - even if I didn't.

"Nope, these are fine too. I think you're good here." Oliver turned away from checking the last of the wards, and I was suddenly aware of how close together we had been standing.

Again.

I took a step backwards, grateful that the space in the hall allowed it, and forced myself to smile at him. "Thanks, Olly."

"No problem," he said lightly.

He reached for the door handle, and a strange kind of fear surged up in me. I was desperate to say something – anything – to get him to stay. So, I said the first thing that popped into my head.

"Stop."

"What?" He turned.

I licked dry lips. "I said, 'do you think I should stop'? Practicing magick, I mean?"

He gave me a long look and then said, "This seems like it's going to be a longer conversation. Why don't we sit down?"

I silently thanked the goddess that I didn't spill hot tea on Oliver as I set the cup down carefully on the table in front of him. My hands were shaking so badly that I whisked them behind my back, out of sight, as soon as the teacup was safely down.

He didn't pass comment on my shaking, he just lifted the cup to his lips, blew on it gently, and sipped the contents with an expression of obvious satisfaction on his face.

"That's better," he said, leaning back on his chair so that the front legs were raised slightly off the ground. "Now then, tell me, why do you think you should stop using your powers?"

I winced at both his question and the position of his chair. I could just imagine what Granny Bright would have said if she could have seen him. Forcing myself to ignore it, I said, "I just feel like I'm putting you all in danger. Let's be honest, I'm the weak link here and you're going out of your way to train me. It's risky. Like Izzy said, I could have exposed you all at the beach."

"But that's only because you didn't know what was going on," Oliver began, but I shook my head, silencing him.

"No, Izzy's right. What kind of witch has to be told not to use her magick in public?" I frowned and blew on my tea. "It's basically rule one."

"Maybe," Oliver conceded, "but I think you're missing something important here."

"What's that?"

"You felt like you didn't have a choice. That girl was in the water, your power was calling to you, and you used it."

I shuddered. Oliver was exactly right, I realised. I had felt as if I had no choice. And that was exactly the fear that had driven me away in the first place.

"But I don't want that!" I said. "My power shouldn't be calling to me, I should be calling to it. It's all the wrong way round. And I don't want to feel as if I have no choice, Olly. That's what happened with —"

I had been about to say, 'with Freddy,' but I stopped myself just in time.

"That's what happened before," I said instead. "In New York."

Oliver looked down into his teacup. "That's why you should stay," he said. "Keep learning. Keep practicing."

This time he did look up, and his eyes met mine. "Your magick was always strong, Alyssa. Even when we were kids. But you haven't used it in years, and now it's breaking out of you. Is it any wonder that it's all a bit undisciplined?"

I nodded slowly. "You think I just need to learn to control it?"

"I do." He reached out and placed a hand over mine. "It's a part of you, whether you like it or not. If you don't at least try to explore it, there will always be something missing. You'll never be fully 'you'. Not really."

I thought again about the version of myself I had been in New York. Always hustling, always on the move. Always, I realised now, trying to outrun something that had been inside of me the whole time. I thought about Freddy, about how he wanted the version of me I had shown to the world.

I wondered whether he had ever been interested in getting to know the real me. Not like Olly, who had only ever wanted the truth.

The heat from Oliver's hand seemed to travel right into the core of me. I wanted, more than anything else, for him to stay with me, for him to keep touching me like that, even if nothing else ever happened between us.

"Oliver," I began, and I could hear how my voice was thick with desire.

His phone rang.

We both froze, and then Oliver withdrew his hand, reaching into his pocket to bring out his phone.

Don't answer it, I pleaded silently.

"Hello?" he said. "Gillian? What's wrong?"

Of course, I thought miserably.

"Yeah of course," Oliver said into the phone. "No, it's no trouble. I'll be setting off in five minutes. See you soon." He hung up and put the phone back into his pocket.

"You have to go?" I asked. Already the heat from his touch was starting to cool.

"Yeah." He looked uncomfortable. "That was Gillian. She's in the area and she's going through a bit of a rough patch, so she's asked me to drop in for a chat."

"You still speak to her then?" I tried to sound casual.

He frowned. "Not every relationship has to end badly,

you know. We've worked really hard to stay on good terms."

"I'm sorry," I said softly. Clearly my attempt to sound casual had failed. "I'm sorry it didn't work out between the two of you. And I'm sorry that I wasn't there for you when it ended."

He shrugged. "It's fine. Sometimes things just don't work out the way you want them to. Gillian and I are friends now, and you and I are friends. It's all for the best."

Friends.

"Mmm," I said, because I didn't think I could manage anything else. "Yes." I nodded vigorously, as if to show him how absolutely, totally, fine I was with the situation – stopping just short of giving him a thumbs up.

"Anyway," Oliver said. "I should go."

"Of course. Thanks again for checking the house."

"Any time. Lock the door behind me, okay? Just to be safe."

I nodded and followed him into the hall. "See you soon," I said, and he smiled at me in return as he left.

I closed the door, locked it, and then leaned against it and waited until I heard the sound of his car reversing back up the drive before I let myself slump to the ground in an untidy heap.

It was only then that I remembered Cameron's warning that none of us should go anywhere alone.

Chapter Ten

"He's fine," Cameron said. "I had a message from him this morning."

I let out a breath I hadn't realised I'd been holding.

"Why?" Cameron frowned, suspicion etched into his features. "What did you think had happened?"

"Nothing really," I said. "It's just that he went to see Gillian last night and -"

"Ah."

"– and I thought afterwards that he probably shouldn't have gone alone."

"Except he wasn't alone," Cameron said, not unkindly.

I sighed. "No. I guess not."

"They're friends."

"I know. He told me."

Cameron looked like he wanted to say more, but then he spread his hands in a 'there you are then' sort of gesture and turned away.

It had been a slow morning, punctuated only with the odd customer who seemed more interested in getting out of the rain than they did in actually buying anything. I watched as Cameron made small talk with them all, noticing the way he managed to put them at ease.

The bell above the door rang again, and Cameron moved as if he was just about to go and speak to the family that had entered, when he stopped and drew his phone from his pocket. It was buzzing audibly.

I couldn't see the name on the screen, but the expression on Cameron's face told me that it was witchcraft-related business.

"I'll be in the back," he told me quietly. Louder, to the customers, he said, "Welcome, folks. Feel free to have a look around and if you need anything just give Alyssa here a shout."

He threw a friendly smile in their direction, and then vanished into the back room, the phone already pressed against his ear.

The family stayed for a long time. They cooed over almost every piece of jewellery in the shop, telling me repeatedly how clever it was to make such lovely things out of sea-glass. I smiled my best smile and agreed with them every time. In the end, they left without buying anything, and I wished them a good day and closed the door behind them, shutting out the wind and the rain along with them.

I turned immediately to the back room.

Cameron was still on the phone, and he didn't look up

as I entered.

"Yes," he said. "I'll ask everyone to be on the lookout. Okay, keep me in the loop though, yeah? See you tonight." He hung up.

I didn't like the way he looked. His face was pale, and there were hard lines forming around his mouth.

"What is it?" I asked.

"That was Jan, the leader of the Scarborough coven," he said. "One of her witches has gone missing."

My stomach felt as if it had leapt into my throat.

"Scarborough?" I said weakly. "But that's so close to here. Do they think … I mean …" I couldn't bring myself to finish the question.

"It's too soon to know anything yet," Cameron said. He checked his watch. "Eleven fifteen. Olly will be on his break in a bit. I'm going to ask him and Izzy to meet us here for lunch. I think we need to talk."

The next forty-five minutes seemed to crawl by. Neither of us felt up to dealing with any more customers, so Cameron put a sign on the door that read, 'Sorry. Closed early'. He spent the time ringing and texting his contacts in the magickal community. I heard him speak to Heather – at length – and to someone named Nate, telling each of them the same thing he had told me; no, he didn't know anything else yet, and yes, he would let them know as soon as he did know something.

With nothing else to do, I took a rag from the back room and began dusting the display cases. I was still working when there was a quiet knock on the door, and I looked up to find Izzy standing outside.

I took the keys from the counter and opened the door.

"Hey," I said, trying to keep my tone light.

"Hey," she said, without looking at me.

"Izzy," Cameron said, emerging from the back room. "Sorry about the dramatics."

"What's happened?" She looked around. "It isn't Olly, is it?"

"No," Cameron said quickly. "He's fine. He's on his way here."

"Then what?"

"Sophie from the Scarborough coven has gone missing. I've just heard from Jan this morning."

"Sophie?" Izzy frowned. "But she's just a kid. How could they let her wander around alone?"

"She's twenty-one, Iz," Cameron said. "And I don't know what precautions they were taking or where they lost touch with her. I don't have all the details yet."

"Twenty-one is just a kid," Izzy said. "Is everyone else alright?"

"All accounted for," Cameron said. "Jan has checked on them all this morning."

"That's something then." Izzy leant against the counter. "Goddess. Sophie." She shook her head as though she was trying to clear it.

"We don't know anything yet," Cameron said. "It could still be nothing. She could have gone off somewhere and forgotten to tell somebody."

Izzy nodded, but slowly, as though she didn't believe him.

She looked so small and afraid, standing against the counter that I wanted to say something to her, to try to ease her mind. I was still searching for the right words when there was another light tap on the door and I looked up to find Oliver standing outside, an expression of concern stencilled across his face.

I unlocked the door again, and he strode through with a brief, "Hi."

He looked around and I watched some of the worry vanish from his face as he realised that we were all there.

"It's Sophie from the Scarborough coven," Izzy said, before Oliver had chance to ask. "She's gone missing."

"Sophie?" He frowned. "Shit." He looked around and then said more quietly, "Scarborough. Shit."

I turned to Cameron. "You're going to Scarborough,

aren't you? To talk to Jan?"

Cameron nodded. "Tonight. I'm going to find out what happened - and whether there's anything we can do to help."

"You're not going alone," Oliver said.

Cameron gave him a weak smile. "I was hoping you might say that, mate," he said.

It was already dark when I heard the car horn beep once outside the house. I locked the door behind me, mindful of stepping too far from the protection of the wards.

Oliver was already out of the car and leaning against it in a manner that made me think he was trying too hard to look casual.

I jogged the few feet to the car, pulling my hood up to cover my hair from the light sea fret that was falling around us.

"Okay?" Oliver asked as I approached.

I nodded. "You?"

"As I can be." He held the door open, and I got in, sliding across to the passenger side.

Izzy was at the wheel, with Cameron in the front passenger seat.

"Hey," Cameron said. He sounded tired, and his voice was raspy, as though he had been doing a lot of talking, and

I realised that he had probably spent most of the afternoon sharing the information about Sophie with anybody he thought might have been able to help – and warning anyone he thought might need to know.

Izzy met my eyes in the rear-view mirror and inclined her head in a slight nod.

I returned the gesture and then busied myself with the seatbelt. "Any news?" I asked Cameron.

"Nothing new." He leaned back against the headrest, shoulders slumped. "I spoke to a few people this afternoon, but no one has seen her."

"I'm sorry, Cam," I said. It had been about what I was expecting, but it was still difficult to hear.

The door slammed next to me as Oliver sat down. "Rain's getting worse," he said.

Izzy nodded. "Bad time of year for it," she agreed.

"Granny Bright used to say, 'you can never trust the weather until after Beltane'," I added, and for a moment I thought I saw Izzy's mouth quirk up at the corners in a quick smile.

"Well, it's not going to get any better anytime soon, so we'd better leave now. Everyone ready?" Izzy said. Without waiting for an answer, she reversed the car back down the drive, executed a perfect three-point turn in the small street, and set off in the direction of Scarborough.

Oliver had been right about the rain. By the time we were ten minutes outside of Whitby it was lashing down on us so hard that I was sure that Izzy would have to pull the car over and wait for it to pass. Instead, despite the dark, the rain, and a thick fog that seemed to have materialised out of nowhere, the small witch only leaned forward a little in her seat, her mouth set in a grim, hard, line and her hands clenched so tightly on the wheel that I could see, even in the dim light of passing cars, how her knuckles had turned white with the force of her grip.

Nobody spoke as Izzy wrestled the car along the road. By the time we reached Scarborough, the fog outside had lifted, but the atmosphere inside the car was thick with tension.

Izzy found an empty space on a street near the sea front. She turned off the engine and let out a loud breath.

Cameron was already opening the door. "This way," he said, striding off into the night on long legs.

I scrambled after him, pulling my hood around my face again. The rain was lighter here than it had been on the road, but it was still unpleasantly cold.

Cameron led us away from the sea front, up several small, winding streets, and up to the door of a pub. "In here," he said, pushing open the door.

The smells that assailed me all at once, reminded me just how long it had been since I had been inside a proper English pub. The trendy bars I used to visit in New York had been impressive, but they were nothing like this. The sweet smell of spilled beer hung in the air, along with the scent of old tobacco that rose up from the wet coats and jackets that had been hung over the old radiators to dry. A musty kind of smell had seeped into the carpets and was lingering in the air, mingling with the scent of old wood and cleaning products drifting up from the bar.

The place was warm – almost too warm after the cold outside – and it was abuzz with the sounds of laughter and talking. In one corner of the room, on a slightly raised platform, a man with a microphone was gamely trying to interest the crowd in some kind of quiz.

Cameron led us through the crowd and along to the end of the bar. There was a door there, and he pushed through it, leading us down a steep flight of stairs.

I had expected a storeroom of some sort, so I was surprised to find a room filled with small tables, chairs, and people. There was a stage raised up at the front of the room, and at least thirty people sitting in the chairs, eyeing the stage expectantly.

"She's still doing the gig?" Oliver asked.

Cameron shrugged. "She always does the Thursday

night gig."

"Even now?" Izzy sounded incredulous and more than a little angry.

"She's keeping to her usual routine," Cameron said. "They all are. Just in case."

Just in case anyone is watching them. I filled in his unspoken words.

Cameron indicated a table near the back of the room, and the four of us sat down, squeezing around it.

Before I could ask any questions, a light above the stage began to flash. The last few people found their seats and dropped into them, just as the lights dimmed and a spotlight appeared on the stage.

Four men and a woman walked out onto the stage, to polite applause from the audience.

"Good evening, ladies and gentlemen," said one of the men, as he took his place at the piano. "Thank you for coming out tonight. We are 'The Five Zephyrs', and we will be with you here for the next hour."

He talked for a couple of minutes, introducing the rest of the band, but I ignored him. I fixed my eyes on the woman; a tall slender dark-haired woman who looked to be in her early fifties. She was beautifully dressed in a dark blue, square necked dress and her hair was pinned up in an elaborate bun. Her makeup was just bold enough that I could see it from the back of the room, but not so overdone that it looked theatrical. She looked every inch the professional, but there was something about her – a kind of heaviness that seemed to have draped itself over her, like a cloak. I felt my heart constrict at the thought of what the woman must be going through – and in such a public setting too.

And then the pianist said, "And of course, our wonderful singer, Ms Jan O'Neill."

And the woman straightened, as if she had physically shucked off her sadness, and smiled at the crowd.

I didn't hear one note of the music after the woman started singing. She had a beautiful voice, strong, and high, and powerful, but that wasn't what held my attention. She seemed to have somehow matched the timbre of her voice to the resonant frequency of the room. It soared above us, filling every corner, every nook and cranny with the sound of her song.

I found that I couldn't look away.

Air witch, I realised.

Although I had never known an air witch that could use her voice quite like that before.

As Jan shifted easily into a high 'e' note for the bridge of the song, she swept her gaze coolly over the audience. Her voice never wavered, never changed, and she hit every note with ease, but all the same, she seemed to be scanning the faces of everyone in the crowd.

I felt, rather than saw, the air witch meet my eyes, and for a moment the power of the song seemed to increase, as if she was singing it to me in particular. Then she moved her gaze away, and I felt the power recede back, like a wave pulling back from the shore.

I let out a breath.

Clever, I thought.

In spite of myself, I enjoyed the rest of the show. When the band left the stage, the audience's reaction was less polite and as close to 'riotous' as they could get for a crowd of thirty people in a pub basement on a weeknight.

"Wow," Izzy said. She was leaning forward in her seat, as if she was trying to get one last glimpse of Jan as the band vanished behind the curtain. "Wow."

Cameron signalled to us to remain in our seats. After a few minutes, the band came out and mingled with those audience members that had stayed behind to chat, or to offer their congratulations. I heard a few people make song requests for next time, and the pianist promised them all he would try to fit them into the set. Everyone in the crowd wanted to speak to Jan. She was gracious to all of them, stopping to chat, inclining her head in thanks at their compliments and even posing for photographs with a couple of them, but I could see that the weariness that she had put aside earlier was back.

When the last of the well-wishers had departed, Jan sunk into a chair at the table next to us.

"Thanks for waiting," she said. Her speaking voice was almost as musical as her singing voice; light and lilting with a slight accent that I couldn't place.

"This is Alyssa," Cameron said, and Jan nodded to me with a small smile.

"How are you doing?" asked Cameron.

The woman sighed heavily. "About as well as can be expected, I think. No one has seen or heard from her." A hint of frustration crept into her voice. "Her parents must have called me six times today, and I can't tell them anything."

"And you've tried all the usual spells to find her."

"Of course."

"And," Cameron hesitated, "has Daphne —"

Jan cut him off. "Nothing," she said. "She tried as soon as the sun set."

Cameron let out a breath. "That's something then," he said. "There's still hope."

Jan nodded, but her gaze was fixed on her hands,

fidgeting in her lap.

"Okay then," Cameron said. "Tell us everything."

"There isn't much to tell. She wasn't at the full moon meet a couple of nights ago. That in itself isn't unusual. She's got exams coming up and she had been stepping back a bit to prepare for them. You know everyone has been assigned a partner or a group at the moment, because of the rumours?"

Cameron nodded.

"Her partner called her the next morning, and when she didn't answer, he went to her flat. She wasn't there and neither of her flat mates had seen her. That's when he raised the alarm."

"So how long had she been missing?"

Jan's voice was angry. "Almost three days by the time anybody realised. It seems that everyone was under the impression that someone else had been with her."

"So, she's been gone..."

"Almost a week," Jan said. "No contact with her family, her friends, or with anyone else in the coven."

Izzy opened her mouth and then closed it again, as if she thought better of whatever it was she had been about to say.

Jan didn't seem to have been looking in Izzy's direction, but she nodded. "You want to know how it is that we could have lost a witch in the current climate, and failed to notice for almost a week," she said, her tone clipped. "And the honest answer is that I don't know. Her partner should have been checking on her, but it seems that he was leaving her alone with her studies." She spread her hands in front of her. "We dropped the ball," she said. "Perhaps we didn't take the rumours seriously enough, but that's all they were – rumours. Until this happened."

Oliver spoke. "Is there anything to make you think that a witch hunter is involved?"

"Not specifically, no. But it's almost unheard of for people to go missing around here, let alone for a witch to go missing. It seems like too much of a coincidence to ignore."

We were all silent for a moment, and then Cameron spoke again. "Okay. We'll keep an eye out and I'll put the word out among my contacts in the other covens. You'll let us know if there's anything else we can do?"

Jan nodded. "Of course. And thank you."

"Do you need a ride home?" Izzy asked.

Jan shook her head. "My car is in the car park, and I have a few of my coven-mates waiting for me at home." She looked Izzy full in the face. "We're taking our precautions much more seriously now." She sounded ashamed. "Nothing is going to happen to anyone else. Not under my watch."

"We don't know that anything has happened to Sophie yet," Cameron said. "She's young, she's got exams coming up. She might have just decided to have a few days away and forgotten to tell anyone."

Jan didn't look as though she believed him. "Let's hope so," she said.

A thought struck me suddenly, and my whole body seemed to flash cold. I sucked in a deep breath. "Do you have a picture of her?" I asked.

"Yes, one second." Jan pulled her phone out of her purse and scrolled. "Here. This is all of us at a picnic last summer. That's Sophie, third from the left." She handed the phone to me.

I took it, mentally preparing myself to see a pale woman with green eyes and long dark hair. A woman who had been in my dreams, begging me for help. In fact, I was so convinced of it, that for a moment I failed to register what Sophie actually looked like; a young woman with an elfin face, framed by a reddish-brown pixie cut.

"Thank you," I said, handing the phone back to Jan, and trying to mask the strange sense of disappointment that I felt as I realised that Sophie was not the woman in my dreams.

That there might be someone else in trouble out there too.

Chapter Eleven

We left Jan, safely in her car, with promises to keep in touch.

The rain had stopped by the time we got back to the car. I slid into the back seat again and fastened my seatbelt. Despite the fact it was barely nine o'clock, I felt drained by the whole endeavour.

Izzy turned on the radio and fiddled with the settings until she found a station she liked; something that played heavy metal and rock. She opened the window a little way and drove, without speaking.

I guessed that Izzy was feeling much the same way I was. I leaned back in my seat and allowed my eyes to flutter closed, trusting that there were enough people in the car that if anything happened one of them would do something about it.

I was woken some time later by the sound of Oliver's voice.

"Hello?"

I sat upright and looked around. I realised that we were almost home, and I had been sleeping for longer that I thought.

Oliver was speaking into his phone. "I can't right now," he said. He checked his watch. "Yes, okay. Half an hour?

Take care." He hung up.

No prizes for guessing who he was talking to there, I thought.

I glanced in the rear-view mirror and was surprised to find Izzy's eyes on me. It was only for a second, and then she flicked her eyes away again.

"You going to see Gillian?" Cameron's tone was casual.

Oliver shook his head. "She's coming to me."

"She knows to be careful though, right?"

"Yeah." Oliver sounded tired.

Cameron swung round in his seat, peering at me as best he could manage. "I don't know about anyone else, but I could use a drink. Fancy a quick one?"

"Can't, mate," Oliver said. "I'll have to get straight back."

Izzy frowned. "We shouldn't split up."

"It'll be fine," Cameron assured her. "There'll be plenty of people around, and Alyssa and I will stick together. You could come with us?" His inflection turned it into a question.

"No," Izzy said. Then her tone softened. "Not tonight, I'm tired. I'll drop Olly off and then I'll head home." Her eyes flicked to mine in the mirror again. "Maybe next time," she said.

Izzy pipped the horn twice as she drove away, leaving

Cameron and I standing in the street near the bottom of the steps to the Abbey. Even in the dark, it towered over us, its presence somehow comforting to me despite all the dark mythology associated with it.

Cameron pushed open the door to a small pub, and I followed him in.

Inside, the place was different from the pub in Scarborough. This one was much smaller, and its floor and walls were panelled in wood. Despite Cameron's assertions that there would be plenty of people around, there were only a few men in their twenties sitting together at the bar, an older couple sharing a bottle of wine in one of the booths, and a barmaid pulling pints behind the bar.

She looked up as we came in. "We've finished serving food for the night."

"That's fine," Cameron said.

My stomach growled, as if on cue.

We took a seat in one of the booths, positioned, I noticed, so that we could both see the door.

"Pint?" Cameron asked.

I considered my empty stomach. "Half, please," I said.

He nodded and went to the bar, returning with drinks, four packets of crisps and two packets of peanuts.

"Best I could do," he said.

I took one of the bags of crisps and tore it open, laying

it on the table so that we could both snack from it. "Thanks," I said.

"Now then," Cameron paused to throw a handful of crisps into his mouth. "Talk."

"What about?"

The look he gave me told me clearly that my attempt to play innocent had failed.

"You've got questions about Olly. And by strange coincidence," he waved his hand as if taking in the room, "Olly isn't here right now. So, ask."

"Is it that obvious?"

"Yes," he said, stuffing another handful of crisps into his mouth.

I sighed, took a long sip of my drink, and then turned my gaze on Cameron.

"Tell me about Gillian," I said.

"So, she was a water witch?" I took another sip of my second drink – my hunger long since forgotten.

"A good one too."

"I guess Olly has a type then." I frowned as I thought of something. "If she was a water witch, why didn't you form a quarter coven with her? You have the other three powers between you."

Cameron shifted in his seat. "We talked about it," he

admitted. "But in the end, it didn't happen."

I considered pressing for more information, but he looked so uncomfortable that I decided against it. Instead, I said, "So, how did it end between Gillian and Olly?"

"Well, I don't have all the details, obviously, but I don't think there was any kind of drastic falling-out. They seemed to just drift apart. She started spending more time with her coven and he started spending more time at work, and then one day he told us they'd decided to call it quits."

I frowned. "That doesn't sound like Oliver."

Cameron shrugged. "I'd guess it was Gillian that drove it. She was pretty close with Izzy as well at one point, but by the time she and Olly broke up, she hadn't been spending much time with any of us."

My stomach twisted. *Poor Izzy.* "She's not from here then? You think she wanted to go back home?"

"Maybe. She was certainly spending a lot more time with her home coven."

"And where is that?"

"Newcastle."

I frowned. "Newcastle? That's not exactly close."

Cameron smiled. "I used to call her 'city witch'," he said, and I found myself unexpectedly jealous of the warmth in his voice. "But you're right, it's a bit of a trek. She and Oliver used to split their time, but I think he found it difficult being away from the countryside. Izzy has some friends in their coven so she used to go with her sometimes, but it must have been tough for Gillian being pulled in two different directions like that."

I nodded. "I can understand that," I said, almost to myself.

We were silent for a moment, both of us draining the last of our drinks.

"Another?" Cameron asked.

"Better not." I was already feeling the effects of a couple of drinks on an empty stomach.

"Shall we then?" he gestured at the door.

I opened my mouth to say 'yes', except that what came out instead was, "They must hate me for coming back."

Cameron, who had been half-way to his feet, dropped back into the chair. "They love you," he said, seriously. "Both of them."

I started to speak, but he held up a hand to stop me.

"They're angry with you," he admitted. "And hurt. And it's going to take some time for them to get over that. But they will get over it." He half-smiled at me. "You didn't expect everything to go back to normal overnight, did you?"

"I guess not. But they're so much angrier than I realised. Especially Izzy." I felt tears beginning to form in my eyes and I rubbed the back of my hand against them, embarrassed.

If Cameron noticed, then he didn't comment on it. Instead, he said, "She went to the funeral, you know."

I didn't need to ask him which funeral. There was only one that mattered.

There had been no warning, no indication that she was sick. One day she was alive and writing me letters - posted air mail, because she refused to use email - and the next, she was gone.

I'd had a phone call from some distant relative, a great uncle I think, although I hadn't paid any attention at the time. All I had heard were the words, "Iona is gone."

"Gone?" I'd asked, stupidly. "What do you mean, 'gone'?"

He'd had to explain to me twice, the poor man, before I understood. Even then, I don't think I really understood it. Granny Bright had been a blazing presence in the world, and I didn't understand that the world could carry on existing without her.

I had been dating Freddy for nearly a year, but I flew back to the UK alone. I don't know whether he would have come with me if I'd asked him to – I didn't ask. I told myself that his job was important, and he only got a few days off a year, that I didn't want him giving up his time to go to a funeral.

Part of me reasoned that he hadn't known Granny Bright. He had never met her – she was just a name in my stories, a set of letters tucked away in my dresser. He had no place there, among the people who had known her, and loved her.

A more honest part of me – a part of me that I stuffed down into the quietest recesses of my mind – didn't want my 'normal' boyfriend spending time around my former magickal community. I'd tried to leave that part of me behind, and I didn't want it to be dredged up again. Especially not around Freddy – the person who felt like my passport to the non-magickal world.

The magickal and non-magickal communities had been out in force for her funeral. They had given her a 'good send-off' as they put it. But I had only been able to focus on the fact that I would never see my grandmother again, never speak to her on the phone, or be scolded by her, or drink tea with her in the bright light of a new morning. I had done exactly what was expected of me on these occasions, I had worn mourning garb, read the eulogy, by some miracle kept the witches separate in my head from the non-witches and managed to say mostly the right things to each group. But that was it. Because I knew that I couldn't stay – not with my shiny new job and my shiny new boyfriend both waiting for me, and especially not now that Granny Bright was gone. In the end I had stayed for four days, during which time I hadn't seen Izzy at all, and I had only seen Oliver in passing, and then I'd left again, leaving my spare keys with Cameron, and heading back to Freddy in the hopes that he could mend my broken heart.

Freddy had proposed to me less than a month later. Even at the time I had wondered whether it was too soon, whether it was some kind of desperate ploy to keep us together. But I was at a crossroad. My only remaining family was gone, and my friends – except for Cam – wanted nothing to do with me. I didn't want to go back to my old life. I didn't even want to think about my old life. So, I accepted his proposal and flung myself forwards, into my new life.

"Izzy was concealed the whole time," Cameron said, his voice breaking through my memories and bringing me back into the room. "But she was there." He smiled ruefully at me. "It might be the only time in my life that I've been jealous of a fire witch. Concealment is one of their more useful abilities. And I think we could all have done with being able to hide ourselves away that day."

"I know," I said, my voice barely above a whisper. "I knew she was there."

He didn't look surprised. "You could sense her."

"Not at first. But then I thought about it, and I knew that nothing in the world could have made Izzy miss Granny Bright's funeral. Not even how she felt about me." I shrugged. "After I'd figured that out, I knew she must be using a concealment spell, and then I sensed her."

"You didn't speak to her though."

"She was grieving," I began, and then I checked myself. "*I* was grieving," I admitted. "And I was afraid. I didn't want to speak to her. Not that day." I crossed my arms in my lap. "Granny Bright would have been furious with me for not making the effort to speak to her. She practically raised Izzy."

I expected Cameron to tell me that I was being too hard on myself, but instead he said. "That makes sense with them both being fire witches. I always wondered about your name. Bright. It's not a name common to water witches."

I shook my head. "No, it's from my mother's side of the family. They all run to fire. Granny Bright was fire, her mother was fire, and her daughter - my mother - was a fire witch too."

"But she wasn't around when you were growing up?"

"Something Izzy and I had in common," I said. "A total

lack of parental interest."

"Then your father must have been a water witch?"

I shrugged. "Must have been. But I wouldn't know. I never knew him, and my mother wouldn't tell us anything about him." I frowned and looked at him. "How do you not know all this already?"

"I never asked," he said. "You always seemed a bit sensitive about it when we were younger, and I didn't think it was my place to pry. Your grandma made us all feel welcome – all of us strays and outcasts." He smiled.

I snorted. "You were hardly an outcast. You have a great relationship with your parents."

"All teenagers are outcasts. They buy into the mythos."

"Especially witches," I agreed.

"It explains why you and Izzy were so close though," he said.

I looked away from him, into the bottom of my empty glass. "Like sisters," I said.

Chapter Twelve

It felt as though I had just dropped off to sleep when I was woken by a loud banging on my front door. I sat bolt upright in bed and then froze, unsure whether I had really heard the sound or whether it had all been in my head.

The noise sounded again, louder this time, as if whoever was outside was getting impatient.

I dragged my tired body from the bed, pulled on an oversized t-shirt, and stomped downstairs. "It better not be someone trying to sell me something," I muttered.

I unlocked the door, and flung it open, completely prepared to give whoever was standing there a thorough telling off for waking me up.

It was Izzy.

"Uh," I said, my protests dying in my throat. "Hi. Is everything okay?"

Izzy looked uncomfortable. After a beat, she seemed to shake it off. "Fine. I'm here for training."

"Okay." I was suddenly very aware of how I must look. I tugged at the t-shirt, trying to move it past my knees. "What are we doing?"

Izzy eyed me. "Have you got running gear?"

"Running gear?" Whatever I had expected her to say, it

hadn't been that.

"Trainers, leggings, sports bra. Running gear."

"Uh, sure. Upstairs." I jerked a thumb back towards the stairs.

Izzy frowned, and for a moment, I thought she might tell me that she knew where the stairs were, but she didn't. Instead, she said, "Go get dressed. We're going for a run."

"I thought you said 'training'?"

"This is training. You need to build your energy up. It's why you keep getting headaches every time you work any magick. It's why you passed out the other night. We can't afford for you to be out of action every time you light a candle."

"That's really more your thing."

Izzy snorted. "Well, whatever it is you water witches do. Run a bath or whatever."

I found myself smiling. "I'll be five minutes while I go and change." I held the door wider, inviting Izzy inside.

She didn't so much as glance into the hall. "I'll be in the car when you're ready," she said.

Izzy led me up a steep flight of stone steps leading away from the centre of town. I was already starting to get out of breath by the time we reached the top. I watched as she leant against a bench and stretched her calves, then I copied her motions, hoping it wasn't too obvious that I didn't know what I was doing. I was much more comfortable with yoga than I was with any kind of cardio, and I couldn't remember the last time I had been for a run.

"Ready?" Izzy asked.

I nodded.

I had expected her to start off slowly, but she ploughed ahead at a dead run. Despite my longer legs, I found myself struggling to keep up.

By the time we had been running for ten minutes, I was beginning to lose my temper. I was tired, I was aching, and Izzy had barely said ten words to me in the hour since she had woken me up. I looked at her form, getting further and further away from me, and made up my mind that if she wanted to play games, I would give as good as I got. Drawing in a deep breath, I set my shoulders and increased my pace, closing the distance between us. My feet slapped against the pavement, and my breath came in a series of loud gasps, but despite the fact that Izzy must have heard me coming, she didn't turn, didn't acknowledge me in any way.

Just when I was almost within touching distance, she turned down a side street and headed towards a little dirt path.

Wrongfooted, I half stumbled, and lost a few feet on her while she made her body turn in the right direction. I carried on running for another minute, but it was clear that Izzy was well ahead of me, and pulling further away with each step.

I stopped, and put one hand on my aching ribs, trying to rub away a stitch that had begun to form there.

"Izzy," I gasped out, and ahead of me, she slowed down. "Please," I managed, and she stopped.

"Need a break?" she asked. Despite her words, I could see that her face was almost as pink as the streaks in her hair, and she too was breathing hard.

I just nodded.

Izzy walked back to me. "Stitch?" she asked, with an expression on her face that might have passed for sympathy.

"Yeah."

"Keep walking. It'll help. Come on, we'll go down this path." She pointed to the path, which I could see led down to the beach. "We'll call it a cool down."

We walked in silence for a few minutes, until my breathing returned to normal, and the pain in my side began to subside.

"Better?" Izzy asked.

I nodded. "Yeah. Thanks." I let out a little laugh. "How is it that you're totally fine and I'm dying?"

"Practice," Izzy said shortly. "I run most days."

"You do? You? The girl who used to forge notes the entire summer to get out of track and field?"

"A lot can change in a decade or so," she said.

I winced. "Okay, I deserved that."

"Yeah," said Izzy. "You did."

"I am sorry, you know," I said. "For whatever it's worth. I know how badly you wanted to be part of a quarter coven, and I understand where you were coming from, it's just that I don't think it's for me. I know it's supposed to be the pinnacle of what every witch wants, but I just —" I stopped. Izzy was giving me a strange look: part confusion and part anger. "What?"

"A quarter coven?" she laughed bitterly. "You think I'm angry that we couldn't form a quarter without you?"

"Weren't you?"

"There *are* other water witches, you know," Izzy said, her words somehow tight. "For that matter there are other earth witches and other air witches too. If all I'd wanted was to be in an elemental coven, don't you think I could have found somebody else to do it with? Surely I could have found three people in the whole world who would be willing to put up with me. Especially for that kind of power."

Power, I thought. Suddenly, it was as if no time at all had passed, as if we were still just teenagers and we were still having the same old argument.

"If we have more power, it'll keep us safe," Izzy had said.

"What's safe about binding ourselves together?" I had shot

back.

"If it's not about the coven, then what is it?" I asked.

Izzy looked at me as if I was stupid. Her mouth worked for a moment, as if she was trying to physically hold the words in. When she finally spoke, they came out in a rush, as though they were bursting out of her. "You left us," she said. "You left Olly – and you broke his heart by the way. You left Cameron. And you left me."

There was such pain in her voice, that I reached out without thinking and gripped her shoulder.

"Izzy," I said softly.

Izzy looked up, full into my face.

Time seemed to slow.

The air around us turned warm and hazy. A white feather, dropped from a passing seagull floated down towards us. As it came close to us, it started to rise, as if it had been propelled upwards on a column of rising warm air. All around, small blades of dried grass and grains of sand began to float upwards as well, driven by the warm air surrounding the two of us.

I let go of Izzy, and the air started to cool. The feather dropped again and blew away, out of sight.

"I'm sorry," I said. "I didn't mean to."

I had expected Izzy to be angry that I had used my powers in public again, but she only shook her head and said, with a kind of wonder in her voice, "I can't believe we can still do that after all this time."

We sat together in the longer tufts of grass overlooking the sea.

"You could have found somebody else, you know," I said. "You would have felt safer that way. Maybe you wouldn't even have to worry about the witch hunter now."

Izzy shook her head. "If anything, that kind of power might have drawn attention to us. It could have brought the witch hunter right here. Besides," she looked away from me, towards the horizon. "I didn't want anybody else. We talked about it, when Oliver married Gillian. We all liked her. I really liked her."

"Cameron told me."

She smiled ruefully. "He didn't tell you why we didn't form a quarter with her."

I frowned, remembering the way Cameron had dodged the question. "No."

"Because of me. I couldn't do it."

"What do you mean you 'couldn't'?"

She shrugged. "Couldn't. Didn't want to. Whatever. Either way, I pulled the brakes on it and that was that." She wrapped her arms around herself, hugging her knees in tight. "I just always had this idea that you might come back

– and if you did then I wanted there to be something for you to come back to." She sighed. "I just didn't expect it to take so long."

I resisted the urge to reach for her again. "How'd Gillian take that?" I asked.

"I don't think she ever knew. It's not like we were planning to make her audition or anything."

"How did Olly take it?"

Izzy looked back at me. "I think he understood," she said.

We walked back the way we had come. My legs were already screaming at me, and I knew that I would be sore tomorrow.

There were a million things I wanted to say to Izzy. I wanted to apologise – again – for leaving, for not understanding why she had been upset, for pretending I hadn't seen her at the funeral. I was only just beginning to realise how many assumptions I had made, how many things I had got wrong. I looked over at her as she walked beside me in silence. She was here. She was talking to me. That was all I needed.

"Will you come in for a cup of tea?" I asked, as we walked up to the house.

Izzy hesitated. "Maybe not today," she said eventually.

"Lot of memories in that house, you know?"

I nodded. "I know what you mean."

"Soon though," Izzy said. She quirked her lips in a smile. "I'll come over in a couple of days and check the wards for you. And we can go for another run – you need the practice."

I groaned theatrically. "My legs are cursing you already," I said. "But I'll be there."

Izzy's smile slipped and she suddenly looked much younger, much more vulnerable. "Don't disappear on me again, okay?" she said, in a voice not much above a whisper.

"I promise," I said. "I'm not going anywhere."

She leaned forward and caught me in an awkward hug. "I'll hold you to it," she said, against my shoulder. "Right." She patted me once on the back and we both let go. "I'm going to go. Fancy a drink with the boys later?"

"Sure," I said, even though I could feel my liver beginning to protest. "I'm at work this afternoon, I'll ask Cameron."

Izzy nodded, gave me a thumbs up and retreated back towards her car.

I gave her a little wave, and pointedly ignored the fact we were very obviously both crying.

I finished work a little early and headed home to get

changed. Cameron and Izzy were already in the pub when I walked through the door. I started to say hello to them, but my greeting died in my throat when I noticed the twin expressions of concern on their faces.

"What's wrong?" I asked, shrugging out of my wet jacket and sliding into the booth alongside Cameron.

"Olly isn't here," Izzy said.

I felt my heart constrict, even as the more logical part of my brain was trying to calculate all of the reasons why the usually dependable Oliver could have been late.

"He isn't all that late, is he?" I said, checking my watch. "It's only quarter past. Maybe he's still at work."

"I haven't heard from him all day," Izzy said.

"Do you usually?"

She nodded. "We do at the moment. Everyone checks in."

Cameron took his phone out of his pocket. "I'm calling the garden centre," he said. "Someone there will know if he's been held up." He raised the phone to his ear and gestured to me to let him out of the booth.

I moved, and Cameron shifted past me and out of the door, talking urgently into his phone.

I shot Izzy a panicked look.

"We don't know anything yet," she said, but there was a fear in her voice that belied her calm words.

I was saved from having to respond by Cameron's reappearance.

"Is he —" I started to ask, but I stopped.

Cameron's face was grim. "He isn't there," he said. "He hasn't been there all day. Olly didn't show up for work this morning."

Chapter Thirteen

"We need to find him," I said. "Can we track his phone?"

"Forget that." Izzy's tone was brisk. She looked at Cameron. "Tracking spell," she said.

He nodded, and as if at some unspoken signal, Izzy rose from the table and they both headed for the door.

I shot up and trailed after them.

"Do you have everything?" Izzy asked as we headed up the street away from the pub.

"Feather, bowl of water, salt, white candles, orange candles, clear quartz, map, scrying chain, picture of Olly." Cameron ticked each item off on his fingers as he spoke. "Am I missing anything?"

"No, that should do it." Izzy increased her pace, and the rest of us sped up in turn. By the time we reached Cameron's flat we were all walking so quickly that we were almost jogging. Cameron opened the door and stalked straight through into the main room. He opened a drawer in the bottom of a bookcase and started rifling through it.

"Help me with this," Izzy said, indicating the sofa.

I grabbed one end of it, Izzy grabbed the other, and we shoved the sofa against one wall, clearing a space in the middle of the room.

"Circle?" Izzy asked, and Cameron nodded without looking up.

"I can do it," I said, glad to have something to contribute.

Izzy tossed me a piece of chalk, and I knelt on the floor, drawing the outline of the circle and taking up as much space as I could manage. I called the guardian powers and felt the circle spring into existence as I finished calling the final one.

"Ready," I said.

"Okay," Cameron said. He entered the circle and knelt on the floor, spreading the items out at various points – the salt at the north, feather at the east, orange candle at the south, bowl of water at the west, and the quartz, map, chain, and the white candle roughly in the centre. "I just need a picture."

"Here," Izzy scrolled through her phone and found a picture of Oliver with Cameron. "This'll work, right?"

"That should do it." He unrolled the map and held the chain over it, then he took a deep breath and closed his eyes.

I recognised the chain – and the bauble on the end of it – as the twin to one of the pieces in Cameron's shop, and I remembered how he had told me that he took commissions for the magickal community. It started moving, as if of its own accord. We watched in silence as it sped up and then eventually attached itself to the map, as though drawn by a magnetic force.

Cameron opened his eyes and peered at the map.

"Ravenscar," he said.

I flicked my eyes to the window, where the rain was already starting to coat the glass. "Gods," I said, almost under my breath.

"Break the circle," Izzy said, quietly. "We have to go."

The rain was heavy by the time Izzy pulled the car up to the gate.

"It's locked," Cameron said. "We'll have to walk from here."

We all climbed out of the car. Cameron opened the boot and took out three torches. "Watch your step," he said. "It's slippery."

We climbed over the gate and hurried up the gravel path.

"What if he's in the house?" I asked, as we passed the small stately home. "We'll never be able to get in there."

"We can circle back to that if we don't find him out here," Cameron said.

Out here. In the rain. And the cold.

"Right," I said, trying to ignore the feeling that seemed to have settled in my chest. "Where do we check first?"

Izzy pointed with her torch. "The gardens are that way."

She pointed in the other direction, towards the top of the hill. "The ruins are up there."

"Do we split up?" I asked. "We can cover more ground that way."

"No," Cameron said.

"But Olly —" I began.

"It isn't safe, Alyssa," he said. "We can't risk anybody else."

"There's no time to argue," Izzy said. "Gardens first."

The gardens, which had always seemed to me by daylight to be so pretty and whimsical, were like a madman's maze after dark. The ground was uneven, sloping upwards at odd angles only to drop back down again with no warning. Half of the hedged walkways seemed to be dead ends – forcing us to retrace our steps through the darkness each time we came across a wall of stone or foliage. Each plant and tree, each nook and cranny on the uneven stone walls, cast strange shadows that seemed to twist and elongate – mocking us as we moved past them with our torches. More than once, I thought I saw something on the ground that was large enough to be a man's body – but each time as I drew nearer to it, it would twist and move away from me – just another shadow caught in the glow of my torch.

By the time we had finished searching the gardens, I felt

as though my heart might be in danger of pounding out of my chest. I was exhausted, wet and cold, and heartsick at the thought of Oliver lying out here alone.

"He's not here," Cameron said, something grim in his voice.

I wanted to scream at the time we had lost searching this place – time that we all knew Oliver might not have.

As one, we turned and looked up the hill towards the dark shape of the old alum works.

"Nothing else for it," Izzy said, setting her shoulders as she turned and marched up the hill.

I followed, trying to keep my torch pointed at the ground in front of Izzy where I hoped it would be the most useful. The ground was saturated with water, and I had to work hard not to slip on the muddy trail.

"Oliver," Cameron called from just behind me. "Can you hear us, mate?"

"Olly," Izzy called. "Where are you?"

I added my voice to theirs, afraid that the wind would carry the sound of it away before it ever reached Oliver.

Without discussing it, we turned right at the top of the hill and made our way into the ruins. Most of them had been razed almost to the ground, but here and there we came across some larger buildings, which blocked the rest of the ruins off from our line of sight. We moved forward, calling

Oliver's name and pointing our torches into the corners of each one of the buildings.

As we rounded a bend, I heard Izzy call out, "Olly", in a completely different tone of voice, and I started forward.

Oliver looked as though he had fallen in an awkward position, half slumped over a pile of rocks and old bricks, his head hanging towards the ground.

Cameron started forward, all but pushing me and Izzy out of the way as he rushed to reach his friend. Carefully, he rolled Oliver onto his back and pressed his fingers against his neck.

I could hardly breathe, and it seemed like an eternity before Cameron said, "He's alive."

"We have to get him warm," Izzy said.

"Olly, can you hear us? We need you to wake up, mate," Cameron said, almost gently.

I knelt by Oliver's body. "He's unconscious," I said. I noticed something in the light of my torch, and I re-positioned myself so that I could look properly. There was something dark pooling at the back of Oliver's head, and when I brought my hand to it, my fingers came away wet with blood.

"Someone hit him," I said, and the strange, forced calm that came out when I spoke did nothing to soothe the sudden burst of rage I felt at the thought that somebody had hurt him.

I looked up and met Cameron's eyes.

"We need to get him out of here," he said. "Help me get him up."

Cameron managed to half lift Oliver up, and I wrapped his arm over my shoulder.

"Got him?" Cameron asked, moving to take Oliver's other arm under his own.

I nodded, already too breathless to speak.

We didn't even make it four steps before I slipped, almost dropping Oliver.

On the other side, Cameron lost his footing, and we went down in a heap – Cameron working to break Oliver's fall with his own body.

I felt the last of my breath leave my lungs with a soft whoosh.

"Try again," Cameron panted.

"No." Izzy helped him up and passed him her torch. "This is no good – he's going to end up getting hurt. Cam, go and get the car and drive it up the back roads. We should be able to reverse it into here."

Cameron gave her a dubious look. "That'll take me at least twenty minutes," he said. He dropped his voice. "We need to get him warm. Right now."

"We've got this," Izzy said with total confidence. "You

go – we'll take care of him."

In a flash, I understood what Izzy was thinking. "Go, Cam," I said. "We can do this." I nodded my head for emphasis. "Hurry."

Cameron shot us one last desperate look, and then he took off back down the hill, moving as quickly as the darkness and the driving rain would allow.

I watched him go, and then I shook myself and turned to Izzy.

She had already rolled Oliver into the recovery position. She stood over him, breathed in and held out her hands to me, palms up. "You can do this," she said.

I placed my hands on Izzy's and felt the connection immediately. The world seemed to slow, until I felt as though I could see each individual raindrop falling around us in the light from my small torch. I reached out with my power until I found Izzy's. Almost imperceptibly at first, the air around us started to heat up. The raindrops dissolved into a heat haze that surrounded us, creating a bubble of warm air that encircled the three of us.

On the ground, Oliver let out a slight moan and then fell silent.

I closed my eyes and tried to keep my focus on my magick. I remembered the lessons my grandmother had given me when I was a child, when it had first become clear that I was going to be 'blessed with the gift' as Granny Bright had put it. The words came back to me clearly now, so clearly that it almost felt as though she might have been standing beside me:

Give your magick a colour, my darling. Give it a texture, a smell, a sound. Learn to 'see' it with every one of your senses and it will always respond to your call.

I focused on those long-ago lessons, picturing the magick within me - seeing it as a winding ribbon of power; silvery-blue and smelling of salt water. I felt the magick surge.

"Easy," Izzy said softly. "Pace yourself."

I nodded, my eyes still closed. I felt myself relax into it – like lying back in warm water. And I allowed the power to envelop us all.

Cameron had been right – it was more than twenty minutes before he could reach us. By the time I heard the whine of the car engine as it reversed towards us, I was shaking badly, and the power was no longer flowing as consistently as it had been. The air kept abruptly cooling again and I was aware of Izzy having to work harder to compensate.

"I've got him," Cameron said, and I opened my eyes, sagging with relief.

He had left the car door open, and light spilled out, pooling on the ground in front of us. A loud beeping sound split the air as the car warned us that the engine was still running.

Working together, and with the last of my strength fading fast, we managed to get Oliver into the back seat of the car. The heating was already on, and Izzy took a blanket from the boot and threw it over him, tucking it up around his chin.

I slid into the back seat, laying Oliver's head on my lap, while Izzy jumped into the front passenger seat.

"Is he okay?" Cameron asked, as he hauled the car into first gear and began to drive it forwards, doing his best to avoid the worst of the deep patches of mud.

"He's okay." Izzy sounded exhausted. "We need to get him home."

"Home?" Cameron glanced at her and then quickly back at the road. "We need to get him to a hospital."

"They'll ask questions we can't answer right now," Izzy said. Her eyes were closed, and I could see how pale she was. "We can't risk it."

"Oliver's the one who knows about healing," Cameron said. "Without him —"

"We'll have to do the best we can," Izzy said.

"He'll be watching the hospital," I added. My voice came

out as a mumble, my words slurred.

"Who will?" Cameron asked sharply.

"The witch hunter," I said. "If he thinks Oliver is still alive, he'll be watching the hospital."

Cameron nodded, once. "Home then," he said.

I managed to stay awake just until he pulled the car off the dirt track and onto a proper paved road, and then I felt something inside me shift, and I slipped instantly into oblivion.

Chapter Fourteen

I woke just as Cameron pulled the car up outside Izzy's house.

Izzy scrambled out and rushed to unlock the door, while Cameron walked to the back of the car, opened the door, and dragged Oliver out, using his own body to steady him.

I draped Oliver's arm over my shoulder again – despite the muscles in my back and sides protesting. With firm ground underneath us, we managed to half-carry half-drag Oliver up the drive and into the house.

"Sofa," Izzy said. "We'll never get him upstairs."

We laid Oliver out on the larger of the living room sofas.

"He needs dry clothes," Cameron said.

"I've got nothing that will fit him here," Izzy said. "Get him out of those wet clothes and I'll get you some blankets to wrap him in. Alyssa and I will go to his house and get him some clothes."

"Herbs too," Cameron said. "He must have some kind of medicine kit.

"Right," Izzy said. She beckoned to me. "Come with me?"

"Of course," I said, trying not to let my eyes flick back to Oliver's unconscious form, lying on the sofa.

Izzy ran upstairs and returned with a pile of blankets. She deposited them on the sofa next to Cameron, and he dug in his pockets coming up with a keyring with several keys on it – each of them painted with a wide stripe of different coloured marker pen.

"It's the green one," he said.

"Naturally," Izzy said, without smiling. "Back soon. Lock the door."

She snatched her car keys from a bowl on the sideboard and set off down the hall and out to the car, while I trailed behind her.

It was a short drive to Oliver's house, and we didn't speak for the duration.

Izzy parked the car in the street and marched up to the front door, using Cameron's key to unlock it.

We walked in to find that all the lights downstairs had been left on – and there was a circle chalked on the floor in the living room.

I bent to examine it. Salt, water, feather, candles, quartz, a map and a piece of twine with a jagged, green crystal tied to the end of it. The same spell that Cameron had cast when he had been trying to find Oliver – only with the twine and crystal in place of Cameron's pendant.

I looked at Izzy. "He was trying to find something?"

"Or someone," she said. "She pointed to where some of the salt had been spilled onto the floor. "Whatever he was doing, he left in a hurry." She seemed to shake herself. "We don't have time to worry about it now. I'll go and find him some clothes. You look around and see if he has a medicine kit anywhere." She set off upstairs without waiting for me to respond.

It was strange being in Oliver's house. I had never seen it before - and there was something about it that felt unlike him. The whole place was painted in shades of magnolia, and the furniture was blocky and modern. Somehow when I pictured Oliver, I had always imagined him in a place with soft shades of green on the wall and vintage wooden furniture. I wondered whether the place was rented or whether this had been Gillian's style. I felt an odd pang of sadness that there was no sign of me anywhere in the house. When I'd left, Oliver's old bedroom had been decorated with images of the two of us.

That was a lifetime ago, I reminded myself.

But then I remembered the spell book he kept at work. Some sign of me had survived after all.

I headed for the kitchen and started checking in the cupboards, but it didn't take me long to realise that Oliver must have separated his witchcraft supplies from his more mundane, everyday items. I searched through cupboard after cupboard, coming up with cups, plates, and tins of food, but nothing that was any use to us.

Finally, in a cupboard next to the back door, I found a small bag of the type that gardeners often use to carry seeds. I unzipped it and found that the various pockets were stuffed full of dried herbs, ointments and tiny jars of coloured liquid.

"Any luck?" Izzy asked, coming into the room with a pile of clothes in her arms.

I held up the bag. "I think this is it."

She inspected the bag and nodded. "That looks right." She hesitated, and for the first time all night she looked uncertain. "Do you think we'll need anything else?"

"I don't think there *is* anything else," I said, hating how significant that sounded.

Izzy straightened. "Let's get back then," she said.

As I walked past the back door, I stopped, my attention caught by something in the garden, lit up by the light spilling from the kitchen window. It was an Erysimum plant, its leaves overflowing from the purple pot in which it stood. I knew without looking that if I had turned that pot upside down, there would be a small symbol carved into the base of it. The plant and the symbol both meant the same thing: fidelity. Oliver had planted it for me – just before I left.

If he dies … I didn't allow myself to finish the thought.

"Alyssa," Izzy called from the hall, and I forced myself to step back into the present moment and follow her out of the door.

It was obvious that Cameron had fallen asleep, but he stirred from his position in the chair opposite Oliver the moment we walked into the room. He regarded us with guilty eyes, but Izzy raised a hand, waving off his apologies before he could speak.

"He looks a little better," she said.

"I'd be happier if we could get some medicine into him." Cameron said.

"Got his bag," Izzy said, holding it up.

"What are the chances he left instructions in there?" Cameron asked.

Izzy sighed and ran a hand through her hair, smoothing it away from her forehead. "I don't know yet," she admitted. "I need to get a hot drink in me before I start looking."

I held out my hand. "I'll look," I said.

Izzy passed me the bag and vanished into the kitchen. Cameron resumed his position watching over Oliver.

I spent several minutes looking through the bag. It was filled with pouches of herbs and potions but there were no notes of any sort. Defeated, I walked into the kitchen to find Izzy.

"There's nothing in there," I began, but I broke off when I saw her face. "Are you okay?" I asked.

"Yeah," Izzy said, wiping at her eyes with the back of her hand. "I'll be alright, I just need a minute."

Her hands were shaking, and I walked over to her and gently took the spoon from her. "I'll make this," I said. "You sit down."

I expected Izzy to argue, but she only nodded and dropped into a chair.

"Thanks," she said. "Been a long night. And it's not over yet." She sighed heavily. "I was really hoping Olly would have left some notes. I … I'm not sure I know what I'm doing, and I don't want to do anything that might make him worse."

I tried not to picture Oliver the way we had found him, lying prone in the rain. I shook my head, clearing the image from my mind.

"You won't," I said. "You've always had good instincts; you'll know if something isn't right."

Before Izzy could respond, the door opened again, and Cameron stepped through.

"How is he?" I asked.

Cameron looked exhausted. "I don't know," he admitted. "His breathing is okay, his skin is a normal colour, and I don't think he's running a temperature, but I can't wake him. It's as if all the energy has been drained out of him."

"Maybe he just needs to sleep?" Izzy suggested. She didn't sound very hopeful. "We could give him until the morning, and then if he's no better…"

"We take him to the hospital," Cameron said firmly. "Witch hunter or no witch hunter. We can't keep him here if he isn't getting any better."

I was only half listening to them. Something Cameron had said was echoing through my mind, nagging at me.

It's as if the energy has been drained out of him.

"I think I might be able to help him," I said abruptly.

Cameron and Izzy both looked at me.

"How?" Izzy asked.

"Do you have any string?" I asked her.

I wrapped one end of the string around Oliver's wrist, and the other end around my own, being careful to wrap more layers around my arm than around Oliver's, and not to wrap any of it too tightly.

I looked from Izzy to Cameron, waiting for one of them to say something.

Izzy looked back at me. "It looks right from what I can tell," she said.

Cameron nodded encouragingly.

I took a deep breath and repeated the words of the spell I had cast with Oliver just a few days earlier – the one we had written together so many years ago:

"Spirits of earth,

Lend your strength to the weak,

Awaken the sleeping,

So mote it be."

This time I didn't need to wonder whether or not it had worked. A soft, green glow surrounded the string, travelling up the length of it until it reached Oliver, where it seemed to melt into his skin.

He sighed, and muttered softly in his sleep.

I was so caught up in watching the magick unfold that I wasn't paying attention to how I was feeling, and the sudden sense of exhaustion took me by surprise.

"That's enough," Cameron said. His eyes were on my face. "Break the connection."

I unwound the string from around my wrist and let it drop. The light faded as I severed my connection to Oliver.

I sagged, and Cameron caught me around the shoulders, easing me back into Izzy's armchair. I wanted to ask whether it worked, whether Oliver was okay, but my eyes were already closing, and I couldn't make myself form the words.

I don't know how long I was out for, but when I came to, it felt as if no time at all had passed. I could hear people moving around me, their voices low as they spoke.

"Hey." Cameron loomed into view above me. "He's awake."

I sat bolt upright in my chair.

In front of me, Oliver was also trying to sit up.

"Stay still," Izzy said gently, putting a hand against his chest. "You got hit on the head."

Oliver winced, nodded, winced again, and lay back down.

"Gillian?" he rasped out.

Izzy, Cameron and I all looked at one another.

"What about her?" Cameron asked.

"Is she okay? Did you find her?"

"At Ravenscar?" Izzy asked.

"She was supposed to be there."

"Olly," Cameron said. "You're not making any sense."

Oliver pushed himself up on one elbow and looked at us. His eyes were troubled, but clear.

"She called me," he said. "And part way through the conversation I heard someone in the room with her. Then she just started screaming and the line went dead. When I tracked her, I got a location for her."

"Ravenscar," Izzy said.

"Yes."

"And you just drove out there without telling us?" Izzy's voice was incredulous. "After everything we've said about staying together and making sure we were safe?"

"I had to," Oliver said. "There wasn't any time to get you involved. Not after what happened with Sophie." He looked at us again. "He has her, doesn't he? The witch hunter has Gillian."

Chapter Fifteen

Silence fell over the room. I felt as if all the air in the place had vanished.

"Not necessarily," I heard Cameron say. "It could be something else."

"Like what?" Oliver asked. "What else could have happened?"

"I don't know." Cameron's voice was calm. "But I don't think we should jump to conclusions until we know more."

"Cam's right," Izzy said. "We should —"

She stopped dead.

"What is it?" I asked, my voice just above a whisper.

"My wards," Izzy hissed. "Something just set them off. Something magickal."

Before anyone else had time to speak, there was a loud knock at the door.

I turned to look at Izzy, my eyes wide. "What do we do?"

Izzy looked at her watch. "It's three in the morning. Who would be knocking at the door at this time?"

Cameron looked from Izzy, to Oliver, to me. "It can't be the witch hunter," he said, sounding uncertain. "A witch hunter wouldn't knock."

There was another loud knock, and from outside, a voice

said, "Izzy. Open the door."

Cameron sprang to his feet. "That's Jan," he said.

He left the room and returned moments later with Jan and another woman, this one wearing a heavy, black cloak.

I looked from Cameron to Izzy and back. His face was grim, and hers turned pale as soon as the witches from the Scarborough coven stepped through the door. Olly half rose and then fell back again.

"Sophie is dead," Jan said, without preamble. Her voice was dull, and she looked as though she had been crying.

"Are you sure?" I asked.

"She's sure," Izzy said. Her voice was flat, defeated.

Jan indicated the woman in the black cloak. "This is Daphne," she said. "She's a spirit walker."

My whole body went cold. *A spirit walker.* A witch who was gifted with the ability to speak to the dead. It was a rare – and terrifying – gift and I had never met a witch who had inherited it before. Without thinking, I inclined my head.

Daphne mirrored my gesture, her face almost unreadable.

"I'm so sorry," Cameron said.

"We're on our way to speak to Sophie's mother now," Jan said. "I wanted to see you to tell you all to be careful." She paused and looked at Oliver. "But it seems as if I might be too late. What happened?"

Oliver told her the story, and Jan's face turned even more wan.

She turned to Daphne with a questioning look in her eyes.

The older woman closed her eyes. Her lips moved as she recited something – a spell for concentration or for invocation, I thought. Finally, she shook her head.

"She is not dead," she said. Her voice sounded like autumn leaves rustling in the wind. "But I cannot tell you where she is."

"Could Sophie?" Oliver's voice was low.

Daphne swivelled to face him, turning grey eyes in his direction. "You ask much," she said, but there was no rebuke in her tone, only a simple statement of fact. No one spoke for a moment, and then she nodded her head and said, "I will need help."

I watched as Izzy set up tall candles at each of the compass points.

Jan drew a circle on the floor in chalk – this one much more elaborate than anything I had seen before, containing glyphs and sigils embedded in the design of the circle itself.

"Are you ready?" Jan asked Daphne, and the older woman nodded.

She raised her arms above her head, closed her eyes and

began to chant, her words growing in volume even as she repeated them.

I could feel the power growing and swirling around us. Every instinct in my body was telling me to run, to get away, to find somewhere safe and hide there until the night was over, but I held fast.

At the moment the chant reached a crescendo, Daphne clapped her hands together, just once, and looked expectantly into the circle.

My mouth dropped open. Where the circle had been drawn on the empty floor, there now stood a girl of no more than twenty-one years old, her reddish-brown hair cropped close to her face. It wasn't like in the movies – the girl was neither solid nor entirely transparent, but instead she was a pale form that seemed to radiate light from her centre. I could just make out that there were items in the room behind her, but I couldn't see them clearly. It was like trying to look through fog.

"Sophie," Jan said, and her voice was filled with pain.

The figure turned and looked at Jan. Her eyes were sad.

"I am sorry, young one," Daphne said. "You have been through a horrible ordeal, and we must ask more of you yet. But a life may well hang in the balance in this world."

Sophie tore her eyes from Jan and faced Daphne. Her expression was sad but resigned. She nodded her head.

"We would ask you to help us find your sister witch, Gillian Ford. Do you know where we can find her?"

The ghost looked frustrated. She opened her mouth several times, but no sound came out. A pained expression crossed her face.

Jan looked every bit as confused as I felt. She turned to Daphne with a quizzical expression on her face, her mouth already opening as she formed a question.

Daphne raised a hand, and Jan fell silent.

"Show me," Daphne said. Her voice was soft but there was something buried underneath it – something dangerous and angry.

Sophie turned and I could see that there was something that caught the light as she moved. I leaned forward, frowning, as I tried to get a closer look.

From the other side of the circle, Izzy let out a sharp gasp, and she half rose to her feet, her face contorted in a mask of pure rage. "She's been bound," she hissed.

The ghost nodded sadly, and turned in a slow circle.

Now that I knew what I was looking for I could see it; thin silver wires that had been wrapped around the girl's torso and wound around her wrists. They almost looked as if they were digging into Sophie's flesh, as if they could injure the ghost even in death.

"Wait," I said. "What's that mark on her arm?"

Sophie's head shot up and she faced me with something like excitement on her face. With a visible effort she raised her arm just enough that I could see the mark that looked like it had been branded into it. Sophie's eyes bored into me, and I got the impression that she was trying to communicate something desperately important.

Taking a piece of chalk, I quickly sketched the glyph onto the floor, making sure I didn't disturb the circle as I drew.

The ghost looked relieved for a moment, and then her expression changed back to one of pain. She dropped her arm back to her side.

"Sophie Kent," Daphne intoned, and her voice no longer sounded like the leaves blowing in the wind, but instead it sounded like it might contain the gale itself. "We release you from this place." As the ghost began to fade, she said, "We will find you, child. We will free you."

I thought I saw something like gratitude on the girl's face before she vanished, leaving only empty air behind her.

Daphne slumped where she stood.

Izzy's face was red, and her eyes were almost as wet as Jan's.

"We'll help," Cameron said. "We'll help you find her."

"No." Jan was weeping openly, the tears streaming down her face as she spoke. "She is – was – a member of our coven and we will find her. Besides," she paused to wipe her face. "You have bigger problems." She indicated the symbol on the ground. "Do you know what that is?"

Cameron crouched over it and his face went pale. "Is that…" he asked and then he stopped as though he couldn't get the words out.

"A spell to drain a witch's power," Jan said. "A very old, and dark form of magick." She looked up. "And one of the few destructive spells that we suspect the witch hunters had access to."

I went cold. "But that means —"

Jan turned to me. "It means that you must find Gillian. As quickly as possible."

Daphne straightened. "We must leave," she said. "The sooner we discharge this unhappy duty with Sophie's mother, the sooner we can begin the hunt for her body. We must remove the binding spell from our sister and bring her home."

"I'm sorry we can't help you to find Gillian," Jan said. "It will take all of you working together if you have a chance of helping her now." She looked at Oliver as though she was going to say something more, but then she appeared to change her mind. "Good luck," she said quietly, before she turned and left the room.

A moment later, the lock on the front door clicked back

into place, and I felt the almost imperceptible buzz of Izzy's wards coming back up.

Izzy looked around the room and asked, "What do we do now?"

"You heard Jan." Oliver's face was pale, but his lips were set in a hard, determined line. "We find Gillian."

Chapter Sixteen

"Okay," Cameron said. "We know that she's alive, so we should be able to track her." He hesitated. "I think Jan's right, I think it's going to take all of us."

"Why?" I asked, almost too quickly.

I saw Izzy raise her head and give me a hard stare.

"I tried to find her earlier." Cam spoke quietly. "While you were at Olly's. And I couldn't find any trace of her."

"That's why you asked Daphne to find her," Oliver said.

"Yes."

"But if we know that she's alive," Izzy began, pushing her hair away from her face.

"Then she must be veiled somehow," Cameron finished.

I felt as if my spine had turned to water. I swore inwardly.

Izzy was looking at me again. "Alyssa," she said, and her voice was hard.

"Olly," Cameron said at the same time. "We need a picture."

Oliver palmed his phone from the table and flicked through it. "Here," he said, handing it to Cameron.

"Alyssa," Izzy said again.

I was about to answer her, to try to explain why the

thought of working a group spell filled me with fear, but then I caught sight of the image on Oliver's phone, and I stopped.

The woman on the phone – Gillian – was the woman from my dreams.

I faced Izzy and without thinking said, "I'll do it. What do you need?"

Izzy's shoulder's sagged and I saw for the first time how afraid she had been that I would say 'no'.

"Come with me," she said, holding out her hand.

I took it, and Izzy led me into the centre of the circle.

"Close your eyes and clear your mind," Izzy said. "Try to concentrate on your powers and on the feelings they invoke."

From outside the circle, I could hear Cameron chanting something in a low, quiet voice. I shut my eyes, shut out everything happening in the outside world, and forced myself to focus on Izzy's words.

"See the world as if you're looking at it from above," Izzy said. Her voice had taken on the same low quiet tone as Cameron's and as I listened to them, it seemed that their voices flowed into one, taking on a meditative, almost droning quality.

I felt my breath slow, felt my heartrate decrease, and the tension seemed to drop from my shoulders.

Cameron finished speaking, and I felt the moment he and Oliver moved inside the circle – almost as if someone had rung a bell in the distance.

Without thinking, I held out both of my hands.

Izzy took one and Oliver took the other, and both of them joined hands with Cameron.

I felt us join together in a second, smaller circle, made up only of the four of us and again, it was as if a bell tolled from far away. I felt my hair lift away from my neck, as though a light breeze had blown through the room. My scalp prickled as energy built up between the four of us. It should have been frightening, but there was something so soothing about it, that I didn't feel afraid.

"She's hidden." Cameron's voice sounded both like him and unlike him – as if I was hearing the person he could one day be, rather than the person he was now.

"Veiled." Oliver sounded older, and the tension that had been present in his voice minutes before seemed to have ebbed away and vanished.

"Go deeper." Izzy sounded calm, in control of herself. "We can pierce the veil."

The view shifted and I found myself looking down on the world as if from a great height.

"Look closer," Izzy said, and it was as if we had zoomed in on a photograph.

I saw the town, the sea sparkling and lit in hues of dark blue and grey as the sun shone down on it.

"There," I said, and I hardly recognised my own voice. Joy fluttered through me. I liked this version of myself, this magickal possibility that spoke with such calmness, such certainty. "She's there." In my mind, I thought I must have pointed, although I never let go of Izzy or Oliver's hands.

"In the cove," Oliver said, and I realised that even though I hadn't moved my hands, he understood me all the same.

"Closer," Cameron said, and the view shifted again.

"She isn't on the beach," Izzy said, and I could hear the frown in her voice. "She's further out. In the sea."

Beside me, Oliver shuddered and broke contact.

The circle dissolved, and around us the larger circle hummed and then dissolved too – breaking the spell.

I opened my eyes, and then immediately blinked them shut again. The world was too bright, too full of colour, even in the semi-darkened space.

"Take a minute," Cameron said. His voice was back to normal.

I nodded without looking up, my fingers pressed over my eyes hard enough that I could see sparks rising in the blackness. I stayed like that for several long moments, taking deep, deliberate breaths. Finally, I opened my eyes again to find Cameron peering into my face.

"Okay?" he asked.

"Yes." I huffed out a breath. "That was … intense."

He squeezed my hand but didn't answer.

I wanted to ask whether the others had ever done anything like that before, whether it was always so intense, but one look at Oliver's face was enough to stop me.

"We know where she is," I said quietly.

"In the sea. She must be being kept on a boat. It's the only thing that makes sense." He straightened. "We have to get to her, before they move the boat, and we lose her again."

Izzy raised a corner of the curtain at the window and stared out. "They won't move her tonight," she said. "It's pitch black out there."

"We need to go," he said again, and I recognised the set of his chin, the stubborn tilt of his head.

"We need a plan," Izzy said, gently. "We can't just go rushing off to find her with no idea of what we're getting ourselves into. How would we even reach her?"

Oliver opened his mouth and then snapped it shut. He sighed and ran a hand through his tousled hair, wincing as he touched a sore spot near the back of his head. He nodded and sank back into his place on the sofa, suddenly looking years older. "You're right," he said, and his voice was rough.

"I know you're right."

I felt the beginnings of a headache starting to encroach on my peripheral vision. "I'm just going to go outside for a minute," I said. "I just need some air."

The door banged lightly behind me as I stepped outside into the little garden. In the early morning stillness it sounded very loud and I flinched, half expecting to hear angry shouts from Izzy's neighbours. Nothing happened, and after a few seconds, I let out the breath I had been holding and leaned against the wall. I massaged my temples in slow circles and tried to make sense of the sounds and images that I had just seen. Each time I blinked, I thought I could see Gillian's face - her green eyes staring into mine, her lips moving as she pleaded with me to save her, her dark hair streaming out around her as she tried to free herself from the water. I shuddered and pulled my cardigan tightly around myself. The rain had stopped, and I focused on allowing the cold to wash over me, allowing the scent of earth after the rain to enter my awareness. It felt necessary after the ritual we had just performed – almost as if the elements were washing away the strangeness of the experience, bringing me back to myself.

"Are you okay?"

Izzy's voice made me jump.

"Sorry," she said. "Do you need a minute?"

"No, stay." I patted the wall next to me, and Izzy moved to sit. "Sorry. That was just … not like anything I've done before."

"I know what you mean," Izzy said, and I noticed that she was paler than usual.

"Iz," I said, hesitantly. "About Gillian. Is there any way I could have met her? Did she go to the same school as us? Did she live around here?"

Izzy shook her head. "No, she's from Newcastle. Oliver met her at some work thing, and I don't think she'd ever been here before they started dating. Why?"

I opened my mouth to try to explain, but before I had chance, the door opened again, and Cameron poked his head out.

"You both okay out here?" he asked.

"Fine," Izzy said. "How's Olly doing?"

Cameron made a non-committal sound. "Frustrated," he said. "But I think I've got an idea. I'm going to give Rachel a call."

Izzy swore, and almost jumped up from the wall. "Why didn't we think of that earlier?" she said, pressing one hand against her forehead as if she too was trying to stave off a headache. She looked at her watch. "Will she pick up if you call her now?"

"Only one way to find out," Cameron said, producing a

phone from his pocket.

Chapter Seventeen

Rachel answered on the fourth ring.

I could hear her voice even on the other end of the phone.

"Hey, Rach, sorry to call so late," Cameron said. "But it's a bit of an emergency. I'm going to put you on speaker phone so you can talk to Izzy as well."

He fumbled with the phone for a moment and then I heard the woman's voice. She sounded tired but alert as she spoke.

"What's going on, Cameron?"

Speaking quickly – and with Izzy making occasional interjections – he explained about Gillian going missing and the fact that we knew she was on a boat

"How?" Rachel asked, and Cameron hesitated.

The woman let out a heavy sigh. "Go on," she said.

"Thanks," Cameron said briefly. "That's most of it. We could direct you to the place, but we need to get there quickly. Oliver is afraid that the man who's taken her will move her before we can get to her if we wait."

"Have you called the police?"

"And tell them what?" Izzy's voice was tart. "That someone is kidnapping and murdering witches?"

There was a long – and pointed - silence on the other end of the phone.

"I'm sorry," Izzy said. "It's been a long night."

"It's okay," Rachel said curtly. "I get it."

"Please, Rach," Cameron said. "Olly's at his wits' end. He went racing off to save her once already. We really need to get out there."

I tried to ignore the pit that opened up in my stomach as he spoke.

The woman on the other end of the phone sighed heavily. "Cameron," she said. "It's not that I don't want to help you. But I can't right now."

"Shit," Cameron said. "You're on call."

"I am. And I can't go rushing off into the night with you – no matter how much of a state Olly might be in. What if something happens? April is a bad month around here; we get kids jumping off the pier, we get people taking their boats out to sea because they don't realise how quickly the weather can turn. If my lifeboat crew needed me, and I didn't pick up, if someone got hurt – or worse – because of me —"

"I understand," Cameron said quietly.

"I'd never be able to forgive myself," Rachel finished, as if he hadn't spoken.

"I'm sorry, Rachel," Cameron said. "I wasn't thinking."

I had never heard him sound so dejected – not even when we had been searching for Oliver earlier. I checked my watch. More than six hours had passed since we first set out for Ravenscar. It felt like days.

"Listen," Rachel said, and her voice was soft. "My shift finishes at six; the day crew take over then. Assuming I don't have to go out tonight, I can be at the harbour at ten past. Meet me there and I'll take you out in the Star." She paused. "Just don't do anything stupid in the meantime, okay? It's not safe out there right now."

I felt a chill go through me. *It's not safe out there right now.* Something about Rachel's words felt deeply, profoundly true. I wondered whether the woman had been speaking only about the weather, or if she could possibly know more than she was saying.

"Go and get some sleep," Rachel said. "We'll leave as soon as we can, I promise."

"You're the best, Rach," Cameron said.

"Go to bed, Cam. You've got a couple of hours before we can do anything. Make the most of it." Rachel rang off without saying goodbye.

Cameron stared at the silent phone in his hand for a moment, as if he was expecting it to spring back to life. Then he seemed to gather himself. "You heard the lady," he said. "We should try to get some sleep."

"I'll tell Oliver," Izzy said.

Cameron grimaced. "He won't like it."

She shrugged. "What choice does he have?" She leaned on the wall a moment longer, regarding us. "I'll get some blankets and pillows set up in the living room. We can all stay in one place tonight. Come in when you're ready."

"She's afraid," I said quietly, when Izzy was out of earshot.

Cameron nodded. "After everything that's happened, she's probably right to be afraid."

"What Rachel said about it not being safe tonight…" I began.

"She isn't a witch." Cameron answered my unspoken question. "But she's got experience with the magickal community, and she's put her neck on the line more than once to keep us safe. She's got good instincts too – if Rachel says something is dangerous then I believe her."

"You think she could be talking about more than just the weather?"

Cameron stared off into the darkness, as if he was trying to see something in the distance. Finally, he turned back to me and said, "I think from now on, we have to assume that we're all in danger until the hunter is dealt with."

When I walked back into the living room, I could see

that Izzy had tried to make the place look as cozy as possible. Her sunniest blankets and duvets were spread around the room – some thrown artfully over the sofa and the armchair, and others spread on the floor, as if she was catering for a sleepover.

I half expected her to offer hot chocolate and a selection of scary movies.

Oliver lay on the bigger of the two sofas. His face was still chalky white, and his eyes were ringed with dark circles, but in spite of that, he was propped up on one elbow and there was a hard set to his jawline. It seemed obvious that he had been arguing with Izzy, who stood a few feet away, red-faced and glaring.

The two of them seemed to snap out of it when they realised that they were no longer alone.

"Everything alright here?" Cameron asked, keeping his tone casual.

"Fine," Izzy said, her voice tight.

"We can't just —" Oliver began.

"How else are you going to get there? Swim?" Izzy said. "It's two hours, Olly."

"In two hours she could be dead."

"I don't think so," I said.

They all turned to look at me.

"He's kept her alive this long. That probably means that

he needs her for something. And then there's the water."

"The water?" Oliver frowned.

"She's a water witch, isn't she? And he's keeping her on a boat. Literally right in the middle of her own element. If he wanted to kill her, why would he do that?"

Cameron nodded slowly. "If he took Sophie for her power," he began, and I tried not to notice how he avoided saying 'killed', "then he probably took Gillian for the same reason. So, he won't hurt her until he's had time to perform the ritual."

"And the water thing?" Izzy asked. "Alyssa's right, it doesn't make any sense."

"Maybe he needs to 'charge' her powers up?" Cameron shrugged. "Maybe he doesn't know that she's a water witch and it's just a coincidence. He could have taken Sophie to the same place. There are too many variables for us to be able to figure it out tonight."

"We need to sleep," I said, as gently as I could. "We're in no shape to mount a rescue mission right now." I crossed the room and put a hand on Oliver's shoulder. "We can't help her like this."

After a moment, he dropped his gaze and nodded.

I thought there might have been something bright shining in his eyes, but I didn't look too carefully, choosing instead to look away.

Izzy took the other sofa. She was the only one of the three of us who was small enough to sleep comfortably on it. Nobody suggested that she sleep in her own bed, or that anyone sleep in her tiny spare room; it was as if we all shared the same unspoken agreement that we were safer if we stayed together.

Cameron offered the armchair to me, and I took it gratefully, twisting my body around until I was leaning into the overstuffed backrest, my legs tucked up underneath me so that I could throw a bright yellow blanket over myself, tucking it under my chin so that I was fully covered. I had just enough time to watch Cameron stretch out on the pile of duvets on the floor, his arms crossed beneath his head, before I felt sleep beginning to descend.

It seemed to me that the dream began almost immediately. This time, I ignored Freddy's pleas, his accusatory words, and went straight into the kitchen of the little apartment, looking for Gillian.

She was standing at the sink, watching as the water flowed out of it, beginning to fill up the space around us.

"Gillian," I said. The water was already up to our ankles and rising fast. "You have to come with me." I held out a hand.

The woman regarded me with wide, green eyes. "You're early," she said. "I didn't know you could do that."

"There's no time. Maybe I can get us out of here this time?"

Gillian shook her head. "You can't change it."

"Why not?"

"It's already happened. Or maybe it's still happening now." She shook her head as if she was trying to clear it. "I don't know; I'm so confused."

The water began rushing from the taps at a much faster rate, filling up the space and drowning out everything in a roar as if from a large waterfall. I only had time to realise that the water was cold – as if we were standing outside – before a tidal wave overtook us, knocking both of us over. I made a grab for Gillian, but she was swept just out of reach. As I struggled in the water, I saw Gillian floating in front of me, her green eyes filled with fear, her dark hair swept out around her, like black ink in the water. The woman opened her mouth, but this time, no sound came out.

"I'll find you," I tried to say. "I'll get you back to him." I couldn't tell whether I'd spoken aloud or not. Everything seemed muffled.

The water grew darker, until all I could see of Gillian were her eyes, standing out vividly against her pale skin.

In the darkness of Izzy's living room, I opened my own eyes and found someone was staring back at me. I almost screamed.

"Hey," Oliver raised a hand and whispered. "It's me. I was just checking on you; I think you were having a bad dream."

I sucked in a deep breath and willed my heart rate to return to normal.

"Sorry," Oliver whispered. "I didn't mean to wake you."

"It's ok."

"Water?"

"What?" I said, at an almost normal volume.

"Shh," he hushed me, indicating Izzy and Cameron with a nod of his head. "I said, 'do you want some water'?"

"Sorry. Yes please."

He turned away and headed towards the kitchen. After a moment, I untangled the blanket from around my legs and followed him.

He moved straight to a cupboard in the corner and took a glass from it. I thought again about how much time the other three had spent together, about how comfortable they were in each other's company, and in each other's houses, and I felt a little pang of regret. It took me a moment to realise that Oliver was holding the glass out towards me.

"Thanks," I said quietly.

I drained it in a few large gulps.

"Another?" he asked.

I shook my head. "Can't sleep?" I asked him.

He sighed heavily. "My brain is whirring," he said. "I just keep thinking about everything and I feel like I can't get it to add up."

"Like there's something we're missing?"

"Yeah."

We were quiet for a moment. The only sounds in the house were the low hum of Izzy's fridge and some light snoring that I thought was probably Cameron in the other room. I took a deep breath.

"We'll find her," I heard myself say. "We'll get her back for you."

He gave me a look that I couldn't interpret. "Lyssa," he said softly. "This is my responsibility. I should have gone to her when she asked me to. If anything happens to her now, it's on me."

"That isn't true," I said. "You couldn't have known."

He shook his head. "Doesn't matter," he said gruffly.

For a moment, I thought he was going to say something else, but then he looked down, sighed, and snapped his mouth shut. I waited, but when it became clear that he wasn't going to tell me anything else, I said, "We should try to get some sleep."

He gave me a sad little smile and led the way back into the living room. He indicated the sofa with a quizzical look, but I smiled and shook my head, taking my place back on the armchair.

I turned away so that I wouldn't have to look at him as he settled back down. As I closed my eyes, I offered up a silent prayer to the goddess that I would manage a couple of hours of uninterrupted sleep.

Chapter Eighteen

I was woken by the sound of the alarm blaring on Izzy's phone. From around the room, I heard the sounds of various groans of protest and then Izzy shut off the alarm.

I sat up, stretching to relieve a cramp in my leg, and rubbing at a sore spot on my neck.

"Okay?" Izzy asked.

She looked, I noticed, a lot more alert than the rest of us. At least she had been able to change into fresh clothes – unlike Oliver, Cameron and I, who were all still wearing the clothes we had slept in.

"Yeah," I managed. "How about you?"

Izzy's lips thinned, and she tilted her head as if she was daring the universe to argue with her. "Ready to go," she said.

Oliver and Cameron were already outside waiting for us. There was a light drizzle falling, and I found that I was glad of it. Despite the coldness of the morning, I felt somehow hot and sticky – as if I needed to wash away the events of the previous few days.

Izzy locked the door and pocketed the key, then she spent a moment with her palm against the door, her eyes closed.

I saw a glyph light up – tiny and momentary – at the bottom of the door and realised that Izzy had been reinforcing the wards on her door. I took that as a good sign – it meant that Izzy believed that we were coming back.

We walked in near silence to the harbour. I found myself looking around as we walked, glancing down into every silent street. It was too early for most people to be up and about – especially in the rain – but I spotted the occasional dog walker and a milk float passed us on the main street. I stared hard at each person I saw, but none of them paid our little group any attention and nobody moved towards us.

When we reached the harbour, Cameron led us straight to a little blue boat moored near the end of the pier. The words 'Lucky Star' were painted in cursive script on the side. A woman in a dark blue jumper stood on the deck. Her dark blonde hair was tied up in a ponytail, and she was in the process of pulling on an orange life jacket. She looked up as we approached and beckoned to us to come on deck.

"Hey, Cameron. Hi,Iz." She nodded to them. "Oliver, I'm so sorry. Cameron filled me in. Listen, if she's out there, we'll find her, okay?"

Oliver nodded and allowed the woman to wrap her arms around him in a brief hug. "Thanks, Rachel. I really appreciate —"

The woman waved away his words. "Of course," she said briskly, patting him on the back, and letting him go. "This must be Alyssa." She stuck out a hand.

"Nice to meet you," I said, automatically. "Sorry about the circumstances though."

"Yes." Rachel regarded me for a moment and then nodded as if she was satisfied with what she saw. "Everyone needs to put on their life jackets, you'll find them in the trunk there." She pointed at the trunk. "Cameron, can you help me cast off."

I leaned over the rails as the boat sped across the water. I had to remind myself to take deep breaths. The queasy feeling in my stomach was starting to catch up to the hot feeling in my head - and the combination was leaving me feeling sick and drained.

All the fun of a hangover without the trouble of having had a drink first.

I leaned into the wind, letting the salt spray wash across my face. The salt stung my lips and I licked them, enjoying the slight tang that seemed to help to settle my stomach just a little.

"How are you doing?" Izzy stood next to me on the deck. "You're looking a bit peaky."

I groaned in response.

"How can you be seasick? You're a water witch!"

I closed my eyes. *Much worse.* I opened them again and tried to fix my gaze on the horizon. "It doesn't work like that. If you stuck your hand in a fire, it would still burn."

Izzy shrugged, allowing the point. "We'll be there soon."

Rachel cut the engine and allowed the boat to idle. "We need to be really careful around here," she said. "The rocks are treacherous and the tides are strong this close to the coast."

"So, probably not many people come out here?" Cameron said.

"Here? They'd have to be crazy. There are shipwrecks on this part of the coast as recently as the 1970s."

"That might explain why he's using this part of the cove as his hideaway then. He wouldn't have to work as hard to hide himself if he could just keep people away from here in the first place."

Rachel nodded, one hand on the wheel. "Makes sense," she said. "I don't suppose you can give me any more detail, can you?"

Cameron looked at Oliver, who closed his eyes and raised his head slightly as though he was looking around.

He shook his head. "Not much," he said. "I can sense

… something. But it's like it's blurry somehow."

If Rachel thought there was anything strange about his statement, she didn't show it. "Okay then," she said. "I'll take us in a standard search pattern. Everyone keep your eyes open and shout if you see anything strange."

She drove the boat in slow circles around the cove, slowing each time she spotted any rocks just below the surface of the waves. On the third pass, she stopped the boat entirely, letting it drift.

"What is it?" Oliver asked.

Rachel raised a hand over her brow, shielding her eyes from the weak light cast by the sun showing through a break in the clouds. "I think there's something over there," she said, pointing. "Some sort of inlet maybe?" She frowned. "That's weird though. I could've sworn I'd checked all of the charts for this place, and it wasn't on any of them."

"That's it then," I said. "I mean, it has to be it," I added, as everyone looked at me.

"Anyone got a read on Gillian?" Cameron asked.

"Nothing," Izzy said.

We all looked at Oliver, who slowly shook his head. "It feels like there should be something, but I can't get a fix on it," he said, and the frustration in his voice tugged at my heart.

Cameron looked at Rachel.

"It's going to be risky," she said. "We'll have to take it slowly."

We all looked at one another.

"Take us in," Cameron said.

The inlet was only just wide enough to accommodate the 'Lucky Star'. I could see the strain on Rachel's face as she tried to navigate the shallows. More than once she swore before pulling the boat to one side or another - and she muttered constantly to herself as she worked.

"…close one…" she said, more than once.

After what seemed like an interminable amount of time, we rounded some rocks sticking out of the water and came across a boat, tied up at the point where the inlet began to widen back out into the sea.

"There!" Izzy practically shouted.

Rachel turned, heading straight for the little craft. "Good place for it," she noted in a detached tone. "That overhang will make it almost invisible from the shore, and no one would come out here looking for it." She turned to Cameron, a serious expression on her face. "Whoever is out here, they know what they're doing. Be careful."

I tried not to look down as the deck swayed below me. I gripped tight to the rail of the 'Lucky Star' with one hand as

I stretched the other hand out towards the other boat, where Oliver and Cameron were already standing on the deck.

"You got this?" Oliver asked, reaching his hand out towards me.

I took it, gripping it far too tight, and then gulped as I took the large step between the two boats, landing on the deck of the blue boat – far too close to where Oliver was standing – with a little yelp that was half terror, half triumph.

"Sorry," I said, taking a step away from him, out of the circle of his arms.

Beside me, Izzy landed on the deck, slid a little and steadied herself.

Rachel gave us a little wave and pulled the boat away, anchoring it a short distance away where it was less likely to be in danger from the rocks. I watched it go and felt the pit in my stomach expand just a little bit more.

Everything about this feels wrong.

"Everybody ready?" Cameron asked in a low voice. "Take it steady, yeah? Everyone stick together and keep your eyes open. Let's start up here and work our way down."

"There's no sign of her up here," Izzy said. "And I don't get a sense that there's a veil up here either. If she's still here, then it's more likely that she's below."

"If?" Oliver said, at the same time as Cameron said, "We should check anyway. There might be some clues here that could help us find her."

"Fine," Oliver said. "But we need to be quick."

It didn't take long. There was no sign of anyone on the deck or in the small wheelhouse, and no signs or clues anywhere.

"Down below?" Cameron said, gesturing at the stairs.

My heart rate sped up. Something was telling me – screaming at me – that there was something terrible downstairs.

We all hesitated. Even Oliver took a beat before he nodded once and headed for the stairs. After a moment, the rest of us followed him down.

Below deck, the small cabin was dark and smelled musty.

Izzy pulled her phone from her pocket and turned on the torch, flashing it around the cabin. The light hit something on the ground and Cameron started forward with a small cry of dismay.

Without a word, Izzy followed him and focused the light more closely on the ground. The white outline of a complicated glyph shone in the torchlight, its curving patterns standing out against the painted wood.

"What is it?" Oliver asked, and his voice sounded choked.

"Olly," Cameron said, something like pleading in his voice.

"What. Is. It?" Oliver asked again, a dangerous gap between each word as he spoke.

"It's the power draining symbol." Cameron looked away.

"Then we're too late. He's got what he wanted from her."

"Maybe not," Izzy said. "It could be from earlier."

"From Sophie?" Oliver asked.

Izzy looked sick. "Yeah."

"Gods," Oliver ran a hand over his hair. "I feel like such a bastard for hoping that it's from Sophie." He broke off, shaking his head.

I found that I could barely concentrate on their conversation anymore. "Guys," I said. "There's something strange. I think she's still here."

Oliver looked up sharply, and I raised a hand placatingly. "I know it doesn't make any sense. I just have this really strong feeling that she's around here somewhere."

"How could you possibly know that?" Oliver asked. "You've never even met her."

"Water witches," Izzy said. "They have strong intuition."

Water.

"Maybe that's it," I said. "Maybe she isn't on the boat anymore. Maybe he's keeping her in the water."

"Could he do that?" Izzy asked, looking at Cameron.

He frowned. "It's theoretically possible. If Gillian's power was strong enough, maybe he could keep her alive in the water."

"She's strong," Oliver said quietly. "And stubborn."

"How would we even check that?" Izzy asked. "Where would we begin?"

I walked to the small window to look outside, and as I did so, the strange humming sound that had been in the background almost like a ringing in my ears, seemed to increase. "Hey," I said, "I think there's something here." I reached out and put my palm against the wall and it felt warm – and there was something else too; a strange sensation almost as if something was pulsing gently behind the wall. "Did anyone check over here?"

The other three looked at each other.

"No," Cameron said. He sounded surprised. "Why didn't we look over there? We checked everywhere else."

"I think —" I began. Before I could finish the sentence, there was a faint change in the air in front of me, like a build-up of static electricity.

"Lyss!" Izzy screamed.

Before I had time to move, Izzy slammed into me -

knocking me over. I fell to the ground, looking up just in time to see something hit Izzy hard enough to send her flying across the cabin.

Chapter Nineteen

Izzy hit the back wall of the cabin with a sick thud. She collapsed to the ground, unmoving.

I tried to move towards her, but the boat rocked violently, and I had to struggle to stay on my feet. Outside, the hull made an ominous scraping sound, followed by a crash so loud that I couldn't believe that we were still afloat.

In front of me, grey smoke appeared, floating slowly around the cabin until it coalesced into an almost solid shape. A woman stepped out from behind it, and the smoke dissolved back into grey mist and then vanished completely.

The woman's cheeks were flushed, and her teeth were bared, as if in a snarl. Her green eyes were narrowed and fixed on me.

My mouth dropped open, but before I could say anything, Oliver stepped forward.

"Gillian!" he said.

The woman rounded on him and smiled a cold smile. "Hello, Olly," she said.

I recognised her voice – it sounded the same in real life as it had in my dream. But the woman standing in front of me was calm and sounded like she was in control, unlike the version in the dream, whose voice had been tight with panic.

"It's okay now," Oliver said, and his voice was tinged with uncertainty. "We're here to rescue you from the witch hunter."

Gillian stared at him and then she threw back her head and laughed. She had a wild, raucous laugh – but it was coloured with something unpleasant.

"There never was any witch hunter," Cameron said slowly. "It was you the whole time."

"You always were the clever one, Cam," Gillian said.

"But all those witches." Oliver looked as if he was going to be sick. "The ones in Liverpool. In York. Gods, Gillian – what about Sophie?"

"What about them? They had something I needed so I took it."

"What? What do you mean? You killed them, Gillian! You killed Sophie! How could you do that? She was your friend!"

"I know." Gillian actually smiled. "That's what made it so easy to get her alone. Just like I did with you, Olly."

"And Izzy?" Oliver indicated the spot on the floor where the young witch still lay without moving.

"She hit her with a fire spell," I said. "Just like she used a fire spell to veil herself once she realised we would be looking for her."

"Sophie was a fire witch," Cameron said. "And that's

what you took from her. You stole her powers and then you killed her."

"I still don't understand why," Oliver said. He sounded utterly drained and defeated.

"Why?" Gillian snarled. "Power, my darling. It's always been about power. That's why I dated you, that's why I married you. I thought eventually you would let me in to your precious coven. But she," Gillian indicated Izzy with a stabbing motion, "wouldn't let me in. She was convinced your little water witch would come back and make you all whole again." She glared at me. "And I guess she was half right. Except that you're not whole, are you? And now you never will be!"

A cold fear shot through me, and I managed to make my way across the swaying cabin, bending down next to Izzy. I put a finger on her throat and after a moment, I managed to find a light pulse beating under the skin.

"She's alive," I said. "But she's hurt. We have to get her out of here."

"Aw, poor Izzy." Gillian laughed that mocking laugh again.

"We'll stop you." Oliver's face had lost his pallor and his jaw was set. "Even if we have to strip your powers from you, the way you did to Sophie."

"You really believe that, don't you?" Gillian said, and her

tone was almost conversational.

Without another word, Oliver moved towards her.

Gillian raised her hands, and I felt the strange static humming fill the air again as she gathered power around her.

Time seemed to simultaneously slow down and speed up, and several things happened all at once.

Cameron shouted Oliver's name and pulled him back by one shoulder, turning him away just before the energy left Gillian's outstretched palms and travelled across the cabin, blowing a hole in one wall.

I threw myself over Izzy's prone form, covering her face and shielding her from the blast.

The boat rocked again, more violently than before, and cold water began to rush in from the hole in the wall.

I sucked in a lungful of air, and in moments the tiny cabin was under water. Opening my eyes, I saw Gillian floating a few feet in front of me. Just like in my dream, her green eyes were open wide and her dark hair was spread out around her, like ink staining the water. Unlike in my dream Gillian wasn't pleading for help – she was laughing.

Oliver was trying to swim towards us, one arm stretched out towards Gillian. Behind him, Cameron was still pulling at his shoulder, a look of desperation etched across his face. He opened his mouth as if he was shouting, and I saw him mouth Oliver's name. Even though Oliver couldn't possibly have heard him, he finally turned away from Gillian and allowed Cameron to pull him away, towards the hatch leading back to the deck. Cameron wrapped both arms around his chest and swam backwards, kicking out with his legs as he dragged Oliver back towards the steps.

As I watched, I realised the cabin was getting darker. The boat was sinking.

I lost sight of Gillian, as I tried desperately to swim upwards, towards the air pocket at the ceiling of the cabin. Unlike Cameron, I wasn't a strong swimmer, and Izzy's weight was enough to drag me back down. I could no longer see Oliver or Cameron and I sent up a silent prayer that they had made it back outside.

Gillian will follow them, I realised. *She already has her water powers and Sophie's fire powers. She doesn't need Izzy or me – she'll leave us here to drown while she goes after Olly and Cameron.*

I pulled again at Izzy's unconscious body, managing to move her a few feet before I felt myself beginning to sink back down. The water was freezing cold, and it seemed to leach the heat from my bones, to steal the strength from my muscles as I struggled in the water.

We're going to die down here!

I thought about how I had never really liked going into the water. As a child, my mother and grandmother had never been comfortable with the element – the opposite of their own – and they had discouraged me from going into the ocean with my friends. I had been happy enough on the shore, I had never needed to be in the water to feel connected to it, and then when I left, I had counted it as a sort of blessing, believing that it would be easier for me to walk away from my connection, from my powers, if I stayed away from the water. You couldn't miss what you'd never known – and I had never really bothered to learn how to swim. Oh, I could paddle about in the shallows happily enough – but I didn't have the first clue how to get myself – or Izzy – out of this situation.

The irony of it. A water witch who's going to drown. A dark little part of me almost wanted to laugh.

Maybe it was the cold and the panic making me think more slowly than usual, but it took me a moment to realise the obvious. I was a water witch. I didn't need to swim.

I gathered the last of my strength. *Please,* I said silently to no one in particular, to anyone who might be listening. *Please let this work.* I tightened my grip on Izzy's waist and closed my eyes. Just like the moment when I had stood in front of the sea, I could feel the water respond to me. I could feel it moving around me, like a living thing. And just like before, the magick did not scare me, instead it felt right, it felt safe. It felt, in spite of everything, as though I was exactly where I was supposed to be.

The power grew inside me, until I could visualise it as a bubble of blue light surrounding my body, surrounding Izzy, keeping us both safe. I held the power for a heartbeat more, and then I released it, pushing it out and using the force of it to propel myself and Izzy upwards, across the cabin and through the hatch.

We hit the deck heavily. The boat was tipping at a crazy angle, leaning towards the water, and we began to slide as soon as we landed. I clung to Izzy as we slid towards the rails, twisting her away so that her body didn't take the impact when we crashed into the side.

"Alyssa!"

I looked down to see that Oliver and Rachel were both in the water, their orange lifejackets bright against the grey waves. The 'Lucky Star' was a few metres away, and I could make out a figure on deck, waving frantically at me.

"You have to jump!" Rachel shouted. "You need to get away from the boat before it goes down."

"Izzy's out cold!" I shouted back.

Rachel swore loudly. "Get her to the lowest part of the boat," she called. "Pass her to us in the water."

I nodded and started moving to where the deck was listing at such a steep angle that it was almost touching the grey waves below.

Oliver and Rachel started swimming to meet us.

"Come on!" Rachel shouted. "We have to get out of here!"

I dragged Izzy to where the deck met the water, held her under the arms, and lowered her down.

"Gently now," Rachel said, reaching up towards us. "Guide her down."

My arms felt as though they might be pulled out of my sockets, but I managed to hold on to Izzy until Rachel shouted, "That's it. I've got her."

Gratefully, I let go and watched as Rachel adjusted her position, floating on her back with Izzy on her chest, propelling them both away from the sinking boat and towards the 'Lucky Star'.

"Your turn," Oliver called. "Jump."

I felt as if the last of my strength had left my body. My legs turned to jelly, and my entire body turned cold. The water suddenly didn't seem so friendly, it seemed vast and terrifying.

I looked down and my eyes met Oliver's.

"I've got you," he said, and he spoke so softly that I didn't know how I could possibly have heard him over the noise of the waves, the sinking boat, and the pounding of my own heart in my ears. But I did hear him.

I hauled myself upright, ignoring the way the deck slipped and sloped underneath me, grabbed the railings and threw myself over them before I had time to change my mind.

I hit the water feet first, vanishing beneath the surface. I had time to notice the way the water formed bubbles round my body, the strange sensation of it rolling against my skin, and then I was up at the surface again, gasping in a deep breath.

"I've got you," Oliver said again, this time right in my ear.

He wrapped his arms around me, under my shoulders, using his strength to keep us both afloat as he treaded water beside me.

"Like this," he said. "Use your legs to push the water away from you, as if you were walking upstairs."

I nodded, too tired to do anything else, and moved my legs the way he'd shown me.

"Good, now do the same with your arms – use your hands to push the water underneath you. Like that, only slower," he added, as I started to splash around in the deep water. "Good. You got it?"

I nodded.

"Okay, I'm going to let go of you so I can help you into the boat."

"Okay." I looked up to find that Rachel was onboard and moving the boat slowly towards us.

Cameron was speaking urgently into the radio, but he shot us a quick glance as he spoke, and I saw the relief flash across his face.

In the boat, Rachel leaned over the edge of the deck, holding out her hand. "Come on," she shouted.

"Ready," Oliver called back. He put his hands around my waist and in one fluid movement, he lifted me out of the water, high enough for Rachel to grab my hands.

With Rachel pulling from the boat and Oliver pushing from behind, they managed to get me onboard.

I landed on my knees on the deck.

"Okay?" Rachel asked, and I nodded.

"Now you, Olly," Rachel shouted, holding out her hand again.

Oliver hesitated.

I realised what he was doing. "Olly!" I shouted. "She's gone. Get in the boat."

Oliver looked around one more time, his dark eyes scanning the water, and then he reached a hand up.

Cameron stopped speaking into the radio, and joined Rachel, waving away my attempts to help. Between them, they dragged Oliver from the water and onto the deck, where he collapsed next to me.

Rachel draped a foil blanket over my shoulders, but I hardly noticed it. I hardly noticed the fact that I had begun shaking violently. Without stopping to thank Rachel, who was busily engaged in finding a blanket for Oliver, I crawled over the deck to where Izzy lay, her head propped up on a pile of life jackets.

"Hey." Izzy's voice was weak, rough.

I opened my mouth to reply, but I found that I couldn't speak. Instead, I let out a small cry of pain, and then I burst into tears.

Izzy held out a hand and I took it, gripping hard as I let the tears slide silently down my cheeks.

And that was how we remained, sitting together, hands joined, as the lifeboat appeared over the horizon.

Chapter Twenty

The corridor had been painted in the same pale green colour as the rest of the building. I grimaced. *It's probably supposed to be calming,* I reasoned, but there was nothing that made me feel less calm than the idea that someone had designed something to 'trick' me into calming down.

After what seemed like an age, I found the room number I had been looking for. The door was open, but I knocked anyway before I walked in.

The room was, mercifully, painted white rather than green. A vase of yellow and orange tulips sat on the windowsill along with a couple of cards, one of them obviously hand made.

Izzy lay in the hospital bed, her arm in a sling and her head propped up on a pile of pillows. Her face was pale, and there were dark circles under her eyes, but she looked alert, and I felt some of the fear lift from my chest.

"How are you feeling?" I asked.

Izzy winced. "Like I got hit by a truck," she admitted.

I felt guilt rise in my chest. "Izzy, I'm so sorry," I said.

She frowned. "Why? What have you got to be sorry about?"

"It's my fault you got hurt. If you hadn't pushed me out

of the way —"

"No one will tell me what happened. Can you fill me in?"

I took a deep breath and then told her everything that happened after she had pushed me out of the way – after she had taken the blast that Gillian had meant for me.

"Sophie," Izzy said, so quietly that I almost missed it. "Damn." She shook her head. "Where's Gillian now?"

"We don't know. Oliver looked for her when we were in the water, but there was no sign of her."

"So, she got away." Izzy didn't phrase it as a question.

"Maybe she went down with the boat?"

"It isn't likely though, is it?" Izzy said. "With Gillian being a water witch and all."

I sighed. "No," I admitted.

We were both silent for a moment, and then Izzy spoke again. "There's something else, isn't there?" she said.

I hesitated, hovering on the edge of the bed.

She shifted across and patted the bed with her good hand.

I sat and allowed her to reach out and take my hand.

"I should have told you this earlier," I said. "But by the time I realised that it was important, we were already right in the middle of it, and I missed my chance."

"Okay," she said slowly. "Tell me about it now then."

I told her everything. All about what had happened with

Freddy, and the nightmares I had suffered ever since – and about how the nightmares had shifted, changed to include the mysterious woman with the dark hair and green eyes.

"Gillian," Izzy said quietly.

I nodded. "Yes. But I didn't realise until I saw the picture on Oliver's phone, the night we cast the spell to try to find her."

"That's why you asked me whether you might know her from somewhere."

"Yes. I was really hoping that you were going to give me a reasonable explanation."

"But I couldn't."

"I meant to tell you," I said quickly. "It's just that Cameron came out to talk to us about calling Rachel, right when I was about to tell you about it. And then everything happened so quickly..."

Izzy squeezed my hand. "It's okay," she said. "Go on."

"There's not much more to tell. Only that when we got on the boat, I knew she was there. It was like I could sense her somehow. I can't explain how."

Izzy was quiet for a moment. "You were the one who found her," she said. "Even though you're the last one who should have known that she was there. I should have been able to see through her veil because of my powers, Olly should have sensed her because he knows her the best.

Even Cameron knows her better than you do. But for some reason there's some kind of connection between the two of you." She paused and closed her eyes, leaning back further into the pillows. "Could it be because you're both water witches?"

"I don't know. Is that something that usually happens? Can you sense other fire witches?"

"No." Izzy didn't open her eyes. "But water witches do have the power of intuition. Maybe that makes a difference."

"Well, right now my powers of intuition are telling me that you need to get some sleep."

Izzy smiled. "Will you be here when I wake up?"

"I'm going to Newcastle with Cameron. Oliver is coming to sit with you for a while. I'll stay until he gets here."

"Newcastle?" Izzy opened her eyes with an obvious effort. "Why? Does Cameron think Gillian is there?"

I hesitated.

"What?" Izzy asked. "What don't I know?"

"Cameron can't get in touch with any of Gillian's coven. We're going to try to track them down, to warn them." Izzy's eyes widened. "But what if Gillian beats you to it? What if she's there right now? You could be walking into a trap."

"I don't … I don't get a sense that she's there," I said.

Izzy closed her eyes again. "I don't like it," she said.

"I know," I replied. "But I feel like I have to do this. I can't really explain that either."

"Be careful," she said. "If you feel anything at all, promise me that you'll get out of there."

"I will." I smiled. "I wouldn't want to get hurt just after you've decided we're going to be friends again."

Izzy somehow managed to quirk an eyebrow without opening her eyes. "Did I say that? It must have been the concussion talking."

"You called me 'Lyss' when you pushed me out of the way," I reminded her. "You haven't called me that in years."

"Yeah well, don't let it go to your head," Izzy said, but she was smiling as she said it.

She slipped into sleep, and I remained on the bed next to her, watching her even breathing, until there was a light tap on the door.

"Hey, Olly," I said, without looking up.

"Did you talk to him?" Cameron asked as we waited at the train station.

I shook my head. "Not really. I updated him on Izzy and then we made small talk for a couple of minutes. Then I left."

Cameron threw me a look of exasperation. "Why not?"

I sighed. "I don't know. It didn't feel like the right time. Not with everything that's been going on."

Because I can still see him there in the water, looking for her. Because I can still see the expression on his face when I told him that she was gone.

Cameron looked like he wanted to say something else, but I was saved from further questions by the arrival of the train.

We made our way into one of the carriages and found seats. On a weekday morning, the train was quiet and neither of us spoke as we sat down opposite each other. We had been travelling for some time, before Cameron said, "There was nothing you could have done, you know."

I hesitated. "I guess I know that really. I just feel … responsible somehow. Does that make any sense?"

"None at all," Cameron said cheerfully. "You didn't do anything wrong. You're not the one who hit Izzy, you're not the one who's been going round pretending to be a witch hunter." He narrowed his eyes in fake suspicion. "Unless you *have* been going round pretending to be a witch hunter."

I held up my hands in a gesture of mock surrender. "Not guilty."

"Hmm. That's just what a guilty person would say."

I allowed myself to smile. I could sense the pain buried

beneath Cameron's jokes, the anger at what Gillian had done, but if my friend wasn't ready to talk about that yet, then I wasn't going to force it. I settled back into my seat and watched greenery blur outside as the train sped past the fields and trees. I was tired, but I didn't want to sleep. I was afraid that I might dream of Gillian again if I did – and I had seen enough of the water witch over the past few days to last me for a lifetime. Eventually though, worn out, I allowed the rocking motion of the train to lull me into a light sleep. I didn't dream – but I did have a vague impression of green eyes looking at me, almost as if they were watching me from afar.

Cameron let me sleep until we pulled into the station at Newcastle, then he woke me.

"Come on, sleepyhead," he said gently. "Time to go."

The image of the green eyes that had plagued me as I slept started to recede, and I followed Cameron as he hopped down onto the platform. I trailed after him without a word, as he navigated through the busy, echoing station and out into the city streets.

I switched back into what I had started to think of as 'city mode' almost as soon as we were on the street; avoiding traffic, dodging cyclists and pedestrians and stepping around everyone who was trying to stop us - to ask us to sign a petition or sell us a booklet of vouchers or a charity subscription. Despite the familiarity of it, I found that there was still something that made me feel uncomfortable. At first, I worried that it might mean that Gillian was lurking nearby, watching us, but I still had no sense of her presence, and the feeling wasn't the same as when I had felt as though someone was following me a few days earlier. Still, I took care to be alert for anyone who might be around – for any strange shadows or shimmers in the air that might suggest a veil. There was nothing. It took me almost thirty minutes to place the feeling of discomfort; it was the same sense of alienation, of wrongness, that I had felt when I first moved to the city. New York hadn't been like where I grew up – I had been used to being surrounded by nature, to being cocooned by it almost. Nature was harder to find in the city. It had taken me a long time before I had been comfortable there, before I had begun to feel the strength of the Hudson at high tide, or to feel the connection to the ever present, ever shifting phases of the moon. When I left home though, that had partly been the point. I had believed that staying far away from nature would help me to walk away from my magick for good. I shook my head, remembering. My powers had only started to awaken a few short weeks ago, and I already knew that I would never really have been able to give them up.

Cameron was giving me a look that suggested he had been trying to get my attention.

"Sorry," I said. "Did you say something?"

"I was just asking whether you were alright. You've gone a bit pale."

"I think it's being in the city." I let out a little laugh that I already knew wouldn't fool him one bit. "I guess I've got used to being around the sea again since I got home."

Home.

There it was. I hadn't realised until I said it that I had started to think of Whitby as home again, but I knew it was true them moment the word was out of my mouth.

Cameron looked pleased, but he didn't comment on it. Instead, he nodded and said, "It can be a big adjustment. We'll be near the river soon, that should help."

As we walked, I thought about Oliver. It was no wonder he didn't want to move here. In fact, he was almost uniquely unsuited to it. A city could be an exciting place for a fire witch, with its endless supply of energy. An air witch could make the adjustment. Even a water witch would be fine (better once they found the nearest river). But an earth witch? Oliver needed greenery around him to thrive. It would be virtually impossible for him to make a home somewhere like this.

"He would have been miserable here." I spoke out loud, without meaning to voice the thought.

"Even ignoring the fact that his wife turned out to be a murderous nightmare, you mean," Cameron said, obviously knowing exactly what I was thinking.

We crossed a bridge and made our way down to the river, passing several bars that hadn't yet opened, and one where the faint strains of music were already audible behind the closed door.

Cameron kept walking, pushing through bushes and brambles until we came to a small cycle path that ran alongside the river. We followed the path until it petered out in front of a building.

"This is it," Cameron said.

The building looked ordinary enough – like a small warehouse or a large disused bar – there was nothing to distinguish it from the other ramshackle buildings that were scattered on the waterfront.

"Anything?" Cameron asked.

I knew he was asking about Gillian. Glancing around to make sure there was no one else present, I risked closing my eyes for a second, and realised that there was something different about the building - a sense of power that emanated from inside it, cutting through the stillness of the air.

"She's not here," I said. "At least, I don't think so. The power from that place is making it difficult to tell."

Cameron followed my gaze with a look of concern. "I know what you mean," he said quietly. "It's almost as if it's leaking somehow." He shook his head. "Right, we go in. But be careful."

We walked slowly to the building. Cameron insisted that we walk around the outside once, checking for anything that looked dangerous, before we went any further. I could feel that the wards were still in place, but nothing about them seemed dangerous, so I ignored them, nodding to Cameron as he stood with one hand pressed against the door.

He raised a finger in a silent instruction to me to wait, and then he leaned on the door and used his weight to swing it open.

Nothing happened. He disappeared inside and then after a few moments I heard his voice: "It's safe. You can come in now."

Inside, the space looked much newer than it had from the outside, but it was clear that it hadn't been used for at least a few days. There was a strange feeling about the place, as though the cold had already begun to settle into it, and there was dust on the floor that hadn't been disturbed.

"There." Cameron pointed at one of the windows.

I followed his gaze and realised that something had been carved into the glass: a small symbol at the bottom of the frame.

"What does it mean?" I asked as we studied it.

"It means there's a hidden message somewhere here. One that only a witch can read."

One that only a witch can read.

I reached out with my powers and began to see that the whirling motes of dust in the air were more than what they appeared to be.

"Cameron," I said.

"I see it."

As we watched, the dust seemed to flow and then settle into a pattern, lit from behind by the dim sunlight coming in through the streaked windows.

> *Coven. We have been betrayed. Scatter and do not use any of the safehouses. Trust no one.*
>
> *- E.*

"E?" I asked after a moment of silence.

"Erika must have left the message." Cameron let out a breath. "At least we know she's alive. Izzy will be glad to hear that."

I felt a pang of sadness. "But their coven."

"Gone." There was a subtle hint of anger in Cameron's voice. "Scattered to the four winds as if they'd never existed. Gillian's destroyed them."

I wanted to ask what would happen to them now, but the look on Cameron's face told me that now was not the time to ask questions.

"We should leave," I said, putting a hand on his arm. "We did what we came here to do."

He nodded, patted my hand, and turned to walk out.

I moved to follow him, and then stopped, overcome with a sudden, familiar feeling of dread.

"Cam," I said, and the words seemed to freeze in my throat. "I think she's here."

"Where?" He wheeled, raising his hands in front of him as if in a defensive position.

"I don't … I can't…" I struggled to calm my racing heart, to get control of my ragged breathing. As I did so, the feeling lessoned, until it became part of the background hum of the place. "It's not her," I said. "At least – she's not here now. But I think maybe she left something behind."

Cameron's face twisted. "Her energy is polluting this place," he said.

"It's more than that. I think perhaps she left some kind of message." Without meaning to, I reached out a hand, my fingers stretching absently towards the door frame.

"Alyssa! Stop!" Cameron shouted.

I froze, looking at my hand as though it didn't quite belong to me, as if it had been acting of its own accord.

"Don't move," he said. "I'll be right back."

He rushed past me and through the door.

I dropped my hand to my side, cradling it in my other hand, as though I was afraid it might act without my consent again.

Cameron came back through the doorway holding a branch from one of the bushes.

"Stand back," he said, and I backed off a few feet.

He scrutinised the doorframe until he found what he was looking for – a small mark about a third of the way up. Then he reached out and pressed the end of the branch against the mark.

There was a loud bang and grey smoke seemed to pour forth.

Cameron leapt back, and I covered my mouth with my hand, choking as the stuff swirled around us.

As if from a long way away, I heard laughter – Gillian's laughter. "Hello, Oliver, my love," her voice said. "I'll be seeing you again very soon."

In the middle of the smoke, Cameron found my hand and he led me outside. We both watched as it dissipated and vanished into nothing.

"How did you know?" I asked, fighting back another coughing fit.

"There's only one person she would leave a message for – and he's an earth witch. I knew she would never let anyone else see that message. I took a gamble that her glyph wouldn't be able to differentiate between Olly's earth powers and something that actually came from the earth."

I went cold for a moment. "If you hadn't stopped me from touching it…"

Cameron grimaced. "It probably wouldn't have been good," he said.

We looked at one another, and despite the patch of warm sunlight we were standing in, I shivered.

"So, she's alive," I said. Somehow, I had never really doubted it, but having it confirmed made it feel different, made it feel real.

Cameron nodded. "She's alive," he said.

Chapter Twenty-One —
Three Weeks Later

The bonfires were burning on the beach and the party was in full swing.

Cameron was dancing round the bonfire with someone that I didn't know. I thought the young witch might have been a member of the Scarborough coven though – they were out in force tonight. Jan was singing with the young guitarist who had been at the first beach party, her voice seeming to cut through the darkness at least as much as the fire did, holding the watching witches captivated as they listened.

"Another?" a quiet voice asked, and I turned to see Heather, the black-clad solitary practitioner from Cameron's shop, holding out a beer in my direction.

I hesitated for a second. I had told myself that I would stop after one beer – I still wasn't convinced of the wisdom of having so many witches in one place with Gillian still unaccounted for – but it was the first time the rather severe looking witch had spoken to me, and I didn't want to be rude.

"Thank you," I said, taking the drink and throwing

Heather a small smile.

"Thank *you*," Heather said, with a slight emphasis. She nodded to me, before she moved away towards a small group of people further up the beach. Although she still hadn't smiled, I was left with the impression that I had passed some sort of unspoken test. Ahead of me, Cameron raised his hand in a little wave that seemed to say, 'I told you so'.

I waved back, taking a small sip of the beer. Everyone seemed to be having fun, but I couldn't shake the feeling that there was something dangerous in the air. I ventured away from the Whitby crowd, and my eye was caught by something a little way away – something that looked like a sign set up against the rocks. I walked over to it, and it was only when I was closer that I saw what it actually was. Someone had set a framed photograph of Sophie on an artist's easel and placed it against the rocks. Strewn about it were small bunches of flowers, feathers, and crystals. People had written poems and blessings on pieces of paper and pinned them below the memorial to the young witch.

I stood and looked at the photograph for a long time. "I'm sorry we didn't figure it out in time to save you," I said quietly.

I felt a light breeze behind me, lifting my hair from my shoulders and I turned just in time to see Daphne emerging from the shadows, her dark hood pushed back from her face and her silver hair shining in the firelight.

"I'm sorry," I said. "I didn't mean to intrude."

The woman gave me a strange look. "Why would you be intruding? The purpose of this is to remember Sophie, and that's what you were doing."

"I didn't even know her."

Daphne shrugged. "You shared a common sisterhood. That is enough."

"I wish we could have done more to save her."

Daphne nodded. "We all do. But she's at peace now."

"You found her…" I hesitated, wanting to avoid saying, 'you found her body'. "You brought her home."

"Yes." Daphne regarded me closely. "She saved your friend, you know." She looked down the beach to where Oliver was standing looking out to sea, a bottle in his hand.

I felt my heart constrict. "She saved Olly? How?"

"The night Gillian lured him to Ravenscar. She planned to kill him and take his powers, but Sophie managed to slip out of her bindings and raise the alarm."

"That was who Olly heard screaming on the phone," I said, thinking out loud. "Not Gillian." I frowned. "That's why she hit him."

"Yes. She was outnumbered and she needed to incapacitate one of them while she dealt with the other."

"And Sophie already knew that Gillian was the one behind it all. She would have blown the whole story if she'd escaped." Rage swept through me as I turned back to stare at the picture. "We'll find her. We'll get justice for you."

Daphne shrugged. "The dead don't care about such things," she said. She put a hand on my shoulder and squeezed gently. "Your job now is to protect the living."

I followed her gaze to where Izzy stood on the edge of the firelight.

"Your friends are in pain," Daphne said. "And you are in pain. You should start healing, together."

"I wouldn't know where to begin," I said, almost to myself.

Daphne smiled a sad smile. "Learn," she said, before she turned and walked away, seeming almost to melt into the shadows in her dark cloak.

"Are you okay?" I asked Izzy. My friend was alert, as if she was expecting to see someone. "You didn't sense Gillian, did you?"

"She won't come here. Not tonight."

I sighed. "I hope you're right. I still don't think it's such a good idea for us all to be together out in the open like this."

"With all the wards we put on this beach? This is

probably the safest place in the country right now."

"But something is still bothering you?"

Izzy gave me a half-smile. "I was hoping that Erika might be here," she admitted. "I know Cameron said that the Newcastle coven have all gone to ground, but I thought maybe she might come under a veil."

"Could she do that? Hold a veil for that long?" I thought about the trip to Newcastle.

"She's strong," Izzy said. "And she might not be that far away." Her face fell again. "We don't know where she is."

"Oh, Iz." I wrapped her in a spontaneous hug. "We'll find her. You'll see her again."

"I hope so."

"We will." I gave her a shrewd look. "I have to meet the woman who my best friend is so enamoured with."

It was difficult to be sure in the firelight, but I could have sworn I saw Izzy blush, just a little.

"Well, what about you?" Izzy said, a hint of mischief in her voice. "Beltane *is* the festival of fertility, you know."

"Izzy!" I gave her a mock punch on the arm.

"What?" Izzy held her hands up, her face the picture of innocence. "It can be the fertility of new ideas and new beginnings as well, Lyss. What did you think I meant?"

I laughed. It felt good to laugh after so long and it struck me suddenly that not too long ago, I had thought that there would be no more moments like this with Izzy. I reached out my hand, and Izzy caught it in hers, squeezing gently.

The guitarist struck up a cheerful tune and several people headed for the biggest of the bonfires.

Izzy pointed at Oliver.

"Go and dance with him," she said, a hint of command in her voice.

"Will you be alright here?"

"Go!" she said, laughing and giving me a playful shove. "Have fun!"

Oliver was still standing alone, at the edge of the water when I approached.

"Hey," I said gently.

"Hey," he replied.

There were hundreds of things I wanted to say to him; I wanted to try to explain why I had left all those years ago, I wanted to apologise about Gillian, I wanted to ask whether he was alright. Instead, I settled for, "May I have this dance?"

There was a moment when I thought he might turn me down, but then he smiled, took my hand, and said, "Why not?"

Together, we raced up the beach and joined the dance.

As Oliver swung me around the fire, I could see

Cameron on the other side of it, laughing with Rachel. I could see Izzy by the rocks, raising her beer in an approving salute. There would be more to do, I knew, not least of which would be figuring out how to help protect us all from Gillian and whatever she had planned next. But for now, there was music, and dancing and fun, and for tonight at least, all was right with the world.

The End

ABOUT THE AUTHOR

Lilian Brooks is a practising pagan, who lives with her partner in a little village in the north of England. When she's not writing, she can usually be found hiking with her sister, hanging out with her coven, and posting pictures of her cat to social media.

Her first book, 'Dormant Magick: The Whitby Witches Book One', was published in June 2022.

You can find out more at:

Instagram: @lilianxbrooks
Twitter: @lilianxbrooks
Facebook: Lilian's Magick Circle

And if you have enjoyed this book (or even if you haven't) please consider leaving a review. Thank you.

ABOUT WHITBY

The town of Whitby in North Yorkshire is, of course, real. Many readers will be familiar with the images of its stark and beautiful abbey, made famous by Bram Stoker's 'Dracula', and by the dozens of films and TV adaptations that followed.

These stories are very much inspired by Whitby, and by nearby Ravenscar which, although smaller and less famous than its sister town, is a fascinating place in its own right.

I've changed some of the details of the places I've described (mainly to allow me to give Alyssa's kitchen and garden more space than your average home in Whitby), but most of the places mentioned here do exist. The little 'sunshine yellow' bakery is real, as are Oliver's garden centre, Cameron's shop, and the pub at the bottom of the stone steps. And while, as far as I know, none of these places are owned or operated by witches, Whitby is a magickal place – and anything is possible!

RISING MAGICK:
THE WHITBY WITCHES BOOK TWO

OUT NOW!

Life has never been more dangerous for Alyssa Bright and her friends. The year is waning, and dark powers are gathering against them. With Halloween approaching and their allies falling by the wayside, will the secrets they unearth bring them closer together, or destroy their fledgling coven forever?